Elizabeth gave a convulsive je
At first, I thought she reall
of her mouth was not vomit bı
The only thing I could compaı
underwater by the female frog: billowing, gelatinous stuff, and lumpy, but with no real substance. Except that this was alive, stretching and easing itself into a snake that reached halfway across the table before rearing up slowly and dissolving in the air.

"Stop it," said Lavinia.

Elizabeth twitched again, and this time, a double stream of ectoplasm rolled out, uncoiling and reaching like a pair of serpents or tentacles. It looked, frankly, quite menacing, and Yang leaned back in his seat away from it. Seemingly, he could not, or would not, let go of the hands of the other two.

The ectoplasm fell apart again into a smoky slush that dribbled off the table in all directions and disintegrated into nothingness. Already, a third and greater wave was coming. Elizabeth's jaws were opened wider than I would have thought possible, as though they were being forced apart from inside, but still she was gargling that low, rhythmic chant.

"Break the circle!" Victor was calm and forceful, but there was urgency in his voice.

"I can't!" said Howard.

Like a man who accidentally takes hold of a high-voltage cable and finds himself unable to let go, the sitters were locked together. The ectoplasm surged out into a great puddle that flexed itself, a grey snail emerging from its shell, sliding forwards, and dividing into triple streams that each wriggled toward Yang…

This book is dedicated to all those who asked what Harry did next

ISBN 978-1-948929-75-2

For information address Crossroad Press at 141 Brayden Dr., Hertford, NC 27944
A Macabre Ink Production - Macabre Ink is an imprint of Crossroad Press.
www.crossroadpress.com

First edition

BROKEN MEATS

Book 2 of the Harry Stubbs Adventures

by David Hambling

Macabre Ink

Before we enter into the subject of the occult art as practised on the West Coast of Africa, it will be well to clear the ground by first considering for a moment what we mean by the much-abused term 'Magic'. There are many definitions of this word; and in bygone ages, it was simply used to designate anything and everything, which was 'not understood of the vulgar'. It will be sufficient for our purpose to define it as the knowledge of certain natural laws which are not merely unknown but absolutely unsuspected by the scientists of Europe and America.

"African Magic," Roslyn D'Onston

Lightly answered the Colonel's son: "Do good to bird and beast,
But count who come for the broken meats before thou makest a feast."

"The Ballad of East and West," Rudyard Kipling

Prologue: Shots in the Dark

Norwood, South London, 1925

Purely by chance, I happened to be at the scene of the shooting that marked the beginning of those extraordinary events. At the time I was as perplexed as everyone else, and did not appreciate the full import of that bizarre incident until much later. Nevertheless, it put me in the fortunate position of being able to recount the whole affair not merely from a ringside seat but from inside the ring, so to speak.

In this narrative, I shall attempt to shed light on matters including the tragedy at the Theosophist Circle, the truth about Yang's ghastly death, and the ultimate fate of the man who called himself Roslyn D'Onston. Some of what I shall recount may sound incredible. I can only say that I report what I witnessed with my own eyes. Whether those eyes are to be believed is beyond my judgement.

It started with Collins, who was, not to put too fine a point on it, an undersized individual. This lack of stature put him at a disadvantage in his chosen occupation. If you have to intimidate others, some solid beef is an important asset. Being well endowed with muscle, I have observed how my presence, when collecting debts, is generally sufficient to settle the matter. If a man knows you can pick him up by his lapels and hurl him across the room, he rarely gives you occasion to do so. Some small men have a particular gift for conveying threat verbally, which makes their size irrelevant. Collins, who lacked verbal as well as physical gifts, was forced to resort to other means. He carried a revolver, and let it be known to all that he carried a revolver.

My quiet drink in the pub was interrupted by a scream from outside then a series of reports like squibs, from the alley outside. This was not, I hasten to add, my regular, the Conquering Hero, but a smaller establishment in the same neighbourhood. I frequent it when I am seeking somewhere less boisterous. It is not unfriendly, but people keep to themselves, and conversations are conducted discreetly.

"That's shooting," said my companion.

Seconds later, Sally burst in, looking distraught. Collins was right behind her with a smoking pistol in his hand. "I've just shot Billy McCann," he said, dropping the gun to the floor.

You couldn't top it for sensation. Within two seconds, the pub was in uproar. Someone took the gun Collins had dropped, and the landlord was telephoning the police. The whole pub was crowding round Collins and Sally or pushing outside to see the body.

"Keep an eye on your wallet," my companion advised. I took his meaning; a pickpocket could not have asked for a better distraction.

To understand the situation you have to know a little of the grubby trade that takes place in the shadow of that pub. Sally, or one of Collins's other women, is often to be found smoking at the entrance to the alleyway. Collins is never very far away, and if a man shows an interest, Collins will materialise to take his money and stand guard while Sally and her customer retire to the deeper shadows.

People sometimes complain, but the landlord says he can't do anything about it. He doesn't let Collins or his women in the pub, but that's just show; Walter has seen Collins slipping folding money to the landlord by the back door. Walter says that even the regulars who pass remarks about Sally and the other women aren't strangers to them. As for me, I make judgement on no man and no woman. We all have to earn our crust. Though, given how modern girls are said to lack any restraint, you would not have thought that the trade would continue to flourish. And after the educational talks on diseases that the army made us listen to, I'm surprised women like that can find customers. I suppose some men have uncontrollable urges. But I make no judgement.

Collins was sitting in a doorway when he heard Sally cry out. He was alarmed, and he had his hand on the revolver in his pocket as he came around the corner. He found a man with Sally and, without any exchange of words, shot him six times at point-blank range. Just like that. As to why he had shot the man rather than remonstrating with him or merely threatening him, the only point on which Collins was clear was that it was Billy McCann.

The other important point to bear in mind was that Billy McCann was already dead.

Billy McCann had died of pneumonia the year before. He always had a weak chest and was prone to coughs, and this one just got worse and worse. Bill was no millionaire who could spend winter in the South of France. A cold spell and double pneumonia carried him off. He was a regular at the pub and had done business with Collins's women. Some of those present had been to McCann's funeral.

The three who had gone out to see the body were back. They said there was no one there, living or dead. There was not even, as far as they could tell, any blood from an injured man.

"Something's not right here," said my companion. I could only agree.

"I shot Billy McCann" was all Collins could say. His face was ashen. If it was acting, it was first-rate. "I had to."

Sally was sitting at a bench, cradling a glass of brandy someone had pressed into her hands, and attention now turned to her. Her rouged cheeks and bright lips were like stage makeup. In that lighting, she was as garish as a painted figurehead.

"What happened, Sal?" the landlord asked, not unkindly. "Who was it?"

She swallowed, and shook her head. When she tried to talk, she broke into sobbing. A minute later, she was still crying, the tears leaving dark streaks down her face. The only words we could make out between sobs were "horrible, horrible."

The police constable arrived. He was an experienced older man who did nothing in a hurry. He took stock of the assembled company, nodding in recognition to a few of us before directing Collins outside to the scene of the crime. The rest of us, counting ourselves as material witnesses, gathered around them.

"So, you were standing hereabouts," said the constable, manoeuvring Collins into position. "And this individual was standing where I am now. About two or three feet away, like this."

"That's right," Collins agreed.

"And you believe that you recognised this individual as the late Mr William McCann."

Collins nodded emphatically.

"You shot him six times."

The constable turned around and used his electric torch to examine the wall behind him. Neither he nor any of those with him could find any bullet marks. Then he crouched down to examine the ground, which was entirely free from splashes of blood.

"It was McCann. But he was huge," Collins said unexpectedly. He looked around for a comparison and pointed at me. "Bigger than him even."

In life, Bill McCann barely came up to my shoulder. This was surely a case of mistaken identity if not sheer fantasy.

"He wouldn't stop coming. I kept shooting until he fell over."

"He's not fallen over now," the constable observed reasonably. When Collins made no reply, the constable indicated Sally, who had also been positioned in the correct spot. "You say you shot him because he was molesting this person."

Collins nodded.

"She doesn't show any signs of injury," said the constable, holding the light close to Sally's face and bare neck. Sally looked down, saying nothing. The constable refrained from asking her any questions.

He looked around and found the landlord. "I don't imagine that the weapon has been preserved."

Collins's revolver, for which he did not possess a certificate, had indeed disappeared. The landlord had wrapped it in a towel and left it behind the bar, but now there was no sign of it.

"I could arrest you for the negligent discharge of a firearm," the constable told Collins. "But under the circumstances, it doesn't seem necessary." He turned to Sally. "I could arrest you too, and you know what for."

Collins and Sally said nothing. Both were blank and shell-shocked.

"Very sorry to trouble you, Officer," said the landlord.

The constable nodded slowly. He raised his voice for the rest of us to hear.

"I don't know exactly what has occurred here, but I will remind you *gentlemen* about the laws regarding creating public nuisance and the licensing of public houses." We were all perfectly silent. "I trust you will not again disturb the constabulary without due cause. Now, drink up and go home. A good evening to you all."

"Never even took his notebook out," observed my companion.

We piled back into the pub, and the landlord declared a round of drinks on the house. The usual rule of quiet, individual conversation was suspended, and there was a brisk trade in speculation about the shooting. There was something feverish in the air; we all sensed that something unpleasant was at hand, and we wanted to keep it away with loud talking—like whistling in the dark to keep the ghosts away.

The conversation was too rapid for me to keep up with. Some people had fertile minds, and the ideas came thick and fast. One theory was that Collins had fired into the air, most likely in an argument with Sally. It was harder to explain why she screamed first or why he would have come into the pub afterwards. Maybe Collins's gun was loaded with blanks; that would have scared off an attacker. Surely, Collins would have been aware of what his gun was loaded with, though—unless there had been some jiggery-pokery, perhaps by Sally. The theories grew more elaborate.

If, for the sake of argument, there had been someone there, and Collins had really shot him, the assailant must have been wearing bulletproof mail. Could any mail withstand six shots at close range? Strong opinions were expressed on both sides of the question, not all of them by men who had been in France and Belgium.

Before long, someone voiced the possibility that had been

hanging in the air all along: that the being Collins had shot had not been human at all but a phantom of Billy McCann. Those who were further into their evening's refreshment, and perhaps of a more religious turn, took the view that McCann had been sent as a spectre or hellish visitation. It was a warning to Collins and Sally to mend their ways. That got a general round of approval. People didn't mind any sort of evil thing out there so long as it wasn't meant for them.

Someone mentioned the Hammersmith Ghost. Then talk turned to Jack the Ripper, from thirty years ago, and how he always eluded the police and everyone out looking for him. Then it was Spring-Heeled Jack, who assaulted a girl on Clapham Common twenty years before that, and was said to be bulletproof. Old stories about supernatural hoaxes and frauds were wheeled out, as well as supposedly genuine cases of hauntings.

One man quoted that celebrated speech from the Bard about there being more things in heaven and earth than were dreamed of in your philosophy, and we all agreed on that. Someone else said there was a lot of trickery and mischief about, and you couldn't believe everything you read in the papers, and we all agreed with that, too.

I was still chewing over these things on my way home when I noticed an old Army greatcoat in a doorway. There was no sign of an owner. I assumed it was some tramp's bedding, and then I saw the holes in the front.

I picked up the coat and brought it to the streetlight where I could see it better. A couple of handfuls of fine dirt—or ash—and pebbles were dislodged in the process. It was an old, stained coat, very much the worse for wear. It smelled of filth and urine. I held it at arm's length.

I counted six scorch marks on the coat, with a fresh bullet hole in the middle of each. It had been shot at close range, but there was no sign of the wearer. There were not even any bloodstains, which led me to doubt if anyone had even been wearing it when it was shot. It looked to me like a practical joke.

The police would not thank me for handing the coat in. They might arrest me for wasting their time with a hoax. I did not want to be laughed at for my gullibility. I could not think of anything to do with it, so I tossed the coat in the doorway and went home to my lodgings.

If you had told me the truth of what had really happened, I would not have believed it.

Chapter One

A Job for Harry Stubbs

It was a lean time for me. After losing my clerical position at Latham and Rowe on account of the Shackleton case, I was not able to get another. My income suffered accordingly.

I was obliged to keep an eye on every penny. The pub was a rare treat for me; I could not afford to have so many evenings out as before nor drink as many pints when I did go out. Arthur Renville had insisted on my taking a share of the money from the Shackleton affair. I kept the money in a cigar box under my mattress. Without regular work, I had to raid that cigar box more and more often. What would happen when it was empty?

I applied for jobs everywhere, but there was not much going. I spent half my days filling in application forms and visiting offices and, occasionally, going for an interview. Men talked about the state of the economy and the devaluation the currency. All I knew was that for every clerical job I went for, there were ten men in the line ahead of me. And while my penmanship and arithmetic were up to scratch, if it was a choice between me and a man who did not look like a heavyweight boxer, the other fellow got the job.

There were too many rumours about firms putting their clerks on part-time or cutting wages. My only real employment was in the debt-collection line. If work ran out there, I'd find myself carrying sandwich boards up and down the street, like so many others.

At its most rewarding, debt collection is a matter of cornering individuals who are quite capable of paying up but prefer not to.

These are men—or, very occasionally, women—who routinely withhold payment as a means of obtaining extended credit or to express dissatisfaction with their creditors. When faced with irresistible force, such a person will produce the money with more or less good grace, not infrequently peeling the notes off a large wad carried on his person.

More often, one has to deal with poor wretches who cannot pay. It's a degrading business for all concerned. I do not wish to become so hardened that I can be nonchalant about pulling the wedding ring off a sobbing woman's finger, as one of my colleagues did on the day of the shooting. Her husband just watched, helpless to intervene or pay up. He was another who had lost his job and had borrowed unwisely. All that distress so some moneylender could get his fifteen per cent.

When you come into the pub, it's not pleasant when people start slinking away because they happen to owe money. People resent you even when you just collect what is owed—as though you have the power to let them off.

Pa would have been happy to take me back in the butcher's shop, but my brother already worked there, and the business would have been stretched to support the three of us. I felt bad enough about the wrapped parcel of choice cuts that was pressed on me every time I dropped by.

"We can't have you fading away," my father joked. But the parcels had become larger, and there was concern in his tone when he asked after my situation.

I spent most evenings at the boxing gymnasium. It was an economical way of passing the time, and hard physical activity was the finest tonic in the world. Being unemployed made me feel less than a man; punching a heavy bag restored me. I was training so hard that there was a rumour I was going to stage a comeback. The rumour was fuelled by my enquiries about getting back into the ring, which I made just to see what the purse would be like. In truth, I did not like the feel of the thing. The fight game was fair and square when there was fame and glory to be won. But just boxing for a bit of money, when a person knew he'd never be champion, was a rank business.

"David versus Goliath is an evergreen fixture," Arthur told

me one morning over a cup of tea at his table at the Electric Cafe. This was not long after that odd shooting. Arthur's table was in the corner farthest from the entrance, where he had a good view of the comings and goings and a back door handy should the need for it arise. "The public love it. They'll always be able to sell tickets for that match. But the thing is, Stubbsy… you're not headed for the Albert Hall. The young David in the other corner, the one working his way up, is who they'll be cheering for. You'll be Goliath."

I could only nod in agreement. Before, I had boxed as the hero. I had been Harry Stubbs, "the Norwood Titan." I could have flown to the moon on the cheers when I won my first big fight. It would be different this time around. It might have been better to be a pantomime monster in the ring than a real one collecting debts, but I did not relish the thought of being jeered by delivery boys, especially after a loss.

There was another point against it that weighed more heavily although Arthur was too tactful to point it out: I was a few years older, a few years slower. My fighting style was well-known. Other fighters had the measure of me and knew my weaknesses. I had stopped fighting professionally after losing a few bouts. If I went in again, I would be losing more. The experience was likely to be as hard on my carcass as my conscience. I could easily wind up as a punch-drunk has-been, trying to persuade a promoter that I was still good for one more match.

"On the other hand," Arthur said, holding up an empty palm, "there is paid employment that doesn't involve any bashing about of your own person or third parties."

Now we were getting to it. The Electric Cafe was where Arthur and those he did business with gathered. I was there because of a communication that I might hear something to my advantage.

Arthur is a consignment man. Shipments that have been written off for one reason or another, but which still possess some market value, pass through his hands. He coordinates a vast network of associates who have vehicles or storage room or pairs of hands that can be used at short notice. On occasion,

I have helped unload crates when he was short staffed, just for some beer money. You meet all sorts of people in the process. The point is that Arthur knows everyone, and everyone knows Arthur. The benefits of his business are spread far and wide.

Your wife's dressmaker may offer her ten yards of genuine Indian Calico at a bargain price; your neighbours might acquire a silver-plate tea service that looks more fancy than they can afford; your cook may always manage to stretch housekeeping and still have a bit of stewing steak left over—perhaps you know some of the beneficiaries of Arthur's network. It's how the common man gets a little bit of his own back, Arthur always says. It puts a little bit of money into the pockets of everyone involved.

Arthur never puts himself forward as a leader. He's no gang boss, and nobody exactly answers to him. But he is universally known as a coordinator of great skill and unflagging energy. He has more worldly wisdom than a whole bench of judges. He is the one we turn to, the man who makes things happen. And if Arthur intimates that someone is making trouble or taking more than his share, word will spread, and bones will be broken on behalf of those who care about the common good.

Because of his connections, Arthur sometimes ends up providing unlikely favours, a procedure that leaves people far and wide obliged to him, people who can be called on as and when needed.

"At this point, I will invite our colleague to join us," said Arthur. He gestured for Reg to join us from another table. Reg, a florid, slow-moving man with a fine walrus moustache and bushy eyebrows to match, pulled up a chair and seated himself by stages.

Reginald Brown had taken early retirement from the colonial service in the Far East. I imagined his job had positioned him in some dusty office with a fan revolving lazily overhead, where he spent long days filling out forms with the infinite slow care that keeps the Empire ticking over. His respectability had not been absolute. It seems he had taken advantage of his situation, although Reg always insisted that he had only accepted the customary "cumshaw," or commission, for doing his job, as refusal would have been an insult. He had not exactly left under a cloud, but they say the sky had not been so very fair on that day, either.

As a result of that premature retirement, Reg's pension was less generous than it might have been. He needed a bit extra, and he gravitated to Arthur, making himself useful in small ways. He was generally reliable if not overly honest. We exchanged pleasantries before Arthur addressed the matter at hand.

"You know Captain Hall of course," he said by way of preamble.

Of course I knew Captain Hall. Everyone did. He was a genuine seafarer, a retired ship's captain who'd sailed tall ships in the old days. On some nights, you could find him in the Conquering Hero, leading the assembled company in a sea shanty. Pretty salty some of those songs were, too, in the unexpurgated versions. Or sometimes old Captain Hall could be persuaded to tell stories, long sailors' yarns of terrific storms and shipwrecks and adventures in far-off ports, with the whole circle gathered around him, holding their breath as the fire burned low.

He knew how to tell a tale—which was not to say I believed everything he said. The captain expected to have drink supplied while he yarned, and the longer he went on, the more his tales were apt to swell up and blossom to ever-greater extravagance—blooming roses watered by rum. I'm an open-minded man, but I draw the line at sea monsters and sunken cities.

"There was a Chinese fellow called Yang, a ship's steward, who sailed with the good captain for years. This Yang is settled in Shanghai now, but he has a nephew—or a cousin or some such—who is travelling to these parts. By which I mean Norwood." He tapped the table for emphasis. "He needs a native guide, as you might say, to help him get around and learn the ways of us English folk. I said, 'I know just the man for the job: Harry Stubbs.'"

"I'm gratified that you should think of me. But I don't know as how I'm specially qualified to guide any visitor anywhere. Why doesn't Captain Hall do it? He's hale enough, isn't he?"

"Well, this is where it gets ticklish. Captain Hall resorted to me because he had some concerns about this visitor. And at this point, I will defer to our colleague here, who was twelve years in Hong Kong and can speak with authority."

"Yang's nephew says he's visiting for religious reasons," said Reg. "In China, claiming they're on what they call 'God-pidgin' is a way of telling others to mind their own business. And in my experience, you have to be very careful when the Chinese don't speak plainly."

"It doesn't ring true, does it?" said Arthur. "He's coming all the way from Shanghai and won't tell his own uncle why. You don't come ten thousand miles unless there's money... but that's not the worst of it. Tell him about this secret society."

"I have a few connections Shanghai way," said Reg. "I cabled them, and it seems Yang is affiliated with the Si Fan Society. It's one of their more important secret societies, and one with its long yellow fingers in a great many plum pies." He tapped his nose.

"A criminal fraternity like the Triads?" I had read about the Chinese gangs in the newspapers and in stories. They were famed for their cruelly creative ways of torturing and killing their enemies, for revenge they exacted decades after the event, and for their profound and devious cunning.

"Oh, no," said Reg hastily. "I'm not calling anybody a criminal, and I don't advise you to, neither. That would be exceedingly tactless. But in China, they have an extra way of doing things that runs alongside the official channels. The government, or governments, are a mess. Official channels run slowly—painfully ruddy slowly, to tell you the truth. But they have these mutual-aid societies, like the Si Fan, with their own unofficial channels, and then it all goes *'chop chop'* — very quickly. They're not really criminal, mostly."

"Reg is being diplomatic," said Arthur. "He's too used to dealing with Chinese. You had it about right with the Triads, Stubbsy, and that's why Captain Hall is chary of getting himself involved. Besides, I don't need to tell you that Shanghai means opium and a few other things besides."

There have been Chinese opium dens in the East End since the last century, or maybe longer. They are only patronised by the Chinese and a few adventurous bohemians. But there has been a fuss about Chinese gangs and white slavery in the papers recently, and hackles have been raised. If you believe what you hear, every Chinese laundry is a front for a crime syndicate bent on kidnapping English girls and shipping them out to a life of debauchery in the Far East.

The East End, like every such community, probably harboured a few Chinese gangsters who preyed on their own. But genuine stories of white slavery were as rare as hens' teeth. I couldn't see the Triads setting up shop in South London with no Asiatic population to work with. But Arthur made his living out of his talent for seeing what others missed and making connections. If he thought there was reason to be worried about the visitor, chances were his hunch was right.

"You just keep an eye on Yang and see that he doesn't get into any trouble. I'll pay you the going rate, of course," he said. "Mainly, though, I'm asking you to do it as a favour to me."

It was a matter of record that I owed Arthur. I was not in a position to refuse him. Besides, paid work was very welcome at that juncture. It bothered me, though, that it sounded like the sort of thing that a fourteen-year-old might have carried off just as well. I said as much.

"You're big for an errand boy," said Arthur, winking at me. "But trust me, this is a heavyweight errand. Call it counterespionage."

"Your Chinaman is a subtle fellow," said Reg. "But we can beat them at that game."

"If I was to get Reg to do it, Yang would tumble him in no time," said Arthur. "But we thought that with your looks, you won't arouse no suspicion."

"What do you want me to do?"

"Be helpful. Show Yang around. I don't know… show him how to get on a tram and whatnot. Get fish-and-chips for him. Take him round the Crystal Palace." Arthur waved his hands in an *and so on* gesture. As if Yang were some country cousin up to London for the day who might be entertained after the usual fashion. "Meanwhile, stick close. Find out who he's talking to. See that he's not doing anything as might prejudice our business interests."

"Why don't we just out with it and ask him what he wants here—make it clear where he stands and where we stand?"

"No, no, no," said Reg. "That won't do. You can't ask straight questions like that, and the Chinese don't answer if you do. Did you know there are no words for 'yes' and 'no' in Mandarin? You've got to do everything with polite circumlocutions. What the Chinese call 'face' is very important. If a man chooses not to tell you something, you choose not to ask. See?"

"It's a funny way of doing things," I objected.

Reg wagged a finger at me. "'East is East and West is West, and never the twain shall meet,'" he quoted sagely. I was to find this was his stock explanation for any puzzling Chinese ways. "It's the only way to deal with them. And mind your Ps and Qs—some of them understand English better than you think. Be circumspect and polite at all times."

"I suppose so," I said.

"And the sooner we get rid of him, the happier I'll be. I've got enough to worry about." Arthur swallowed his tea as though it tasted bad and turned to me. "This business with Collins, blazing away like the Wild West, getting the police called in. We can't be having that sort of harum-scarum behaviour round here. Ruins it for all of us."

I told him about the greatcoat with the bullet holes, but apparently, he already knew about it. It had been stolen off the back of a tramp called Slingsby an hour before the shooting, while the man was comatose on cheap gin. Slingsby knew nothing about the shooting and was equally indignant at the theft and the bullet holes.

"It's all tomfoolery," said Arthur. "Some people haven't got the sense to realise that actions have consequences. I gave Collins notice to pack his bags and clear out."

"What about Sally – what will she do?"

"Already seen to. I got them to take her in at Virgo Fidelis. She's a nervous wreck, poor woman."

"A nun? Surely…"

"No, Stubbsy, not a nun. She'll be scrubbing floors or something. Doing her penance."

"Funny business, that shooting," said Reg with a sidelong

look at Arthur as if he were fishing for information.

"Funny, and very unprofitable at that," said Arthur darkly. "Why is it always me clearing up the messes left by other people? Why do I bother?"

Reg and I tactfully remained silent.

"One funny thing about it that did occur to me," Arthur said, brightening a little. "Bill McCann was always very smart, very well turned out. He wouldn't be seen dead in Slingsby's old greatcoat."

Chapter Two

The Visitor Arrives

I like to have things cut and dried. The Royal Artillery suited me. When it comes to lugging shells from one place to another, I'm as good a man as you're likely to find, and stronger than most. I can follow plain orders to the letter. When I have to rely on my own initiative, I'm a traveller without a map.

Arthur and Reg wanted to promote me to the Intelligence Corps, and I had to live up to it. After all, I said I wanted a job that required some brainwork, so I could not complain. It was with no small amount of trepidation that I turned up at the railway station. I arrived in good time and occupied myself at a bench in the waiting room, perusing a book of poetry by Mr Robert Browning. Browning had inspired Sir Ernest Shackleton, and I wanted inspiration.

I could not concentrate on the fine writing. The hands of the station clock seemed to be fixed in place; every time I looked up, it was still 2:43. The experience was as bad as going for a job interview, and a deal worse than stepping into the ring.

My one good suit was something the worse for wear, having already been turned. It would pass at a pinch but was hardly smart. My bowler had been dented in a scuffle with a debtor and had never quite recovered. Nor could any amount of polishing disguise my scuffed shoes.

I thought I would have the advantage of Mr Yang, and so I did. I spotted him from the other side of the concourse, not because he was Chinese but because of his distinctive attire. If I had half expected a robed figure off a Willow Pattern plate, surrounded by cranes and pagodas, the image was dispelled at once.

Mr Yang was clad in an immaculate cream linen suit, with cream leather shoes and spats, topped off with a Derby hat in the same shade. The effect was set off by a pale-blue shirt and a dark-blue tie, and gold gleamed from his tiepin. He stood with one hand in his jacket pocket and a light overcoat over the other arm. A neatly trimmed goatee completed the look; he was posed as perfectly as a fashion plate. If you could say a man was beautiful, then Yang looked beautiful. Not foppish, but sharp as a new razor. And he held himself at a distance, as far above everyone else as a statue on a plinth.

Yang looked through the gawking people as though they were no more than wraiths of steam that swam around him. And in spite of the smoke and soot from the train, there was no trace of smut on him. The elements themselves seemed to respect him.

Yang was no more than a bantamweight, and maybe not even that, but he had the presence of a man six feet tall. He stood with the certainty of a high official surrounded by invisible attendants ready to drag off for execution anyone who crossed his path.

His eyes took focus, and he looked in my direction as I approached. Those eyes! I almost stopped in my tracks. He seemed to have a third eyelid, like a bird, so that his gaze became suddenly penetrating. That look was disconcerting even for an instant.

"Mr Yang, I presume," I said, raising my hat. "I'm Harry Stubbs. Welcome to Norwood. Captain Hall sends his compliments."

"So I understand," he said without offering a hand. There was no smile, no more warmth than if I were a bus he had been waiting for.

"Allow me to show you to your hotel." His steamer trunks would arrive on the next train, and he only had light luggage with him: two suitcases, a valise, and a round wicker basket. I gathered them up.

"Are there no porters here?" he asked.

I suspected that the porters might not give a Chinese gentleman's luggage quite the respect that was due. I did not want Yang to get a bad impression of England. "No need, sir. These don't weigh anything."

I lifted the cases high to illustrate my point. Something shifted in the wicker basket, and two green eyes looked out at me through a lattice—hard, feline eyes, like matched emeralds. They blinked once, as if in warning, but there was no meow. I lowered the basket carefully.

It was a scant two hundred yards to the Tulse Hill Hotel from the station. I pointed out the local landmarks, which Mr Yang barely acknowledged. He was not excited to be in the beating heart of the Empire, our great metropolis from which the world is ruled. The streets full of motorcars and buses and the bright modern shop fronts with their plate-glass windows seemed beneath his notice. London may not have been very exotic after Shanghai's streets, which I imagined to be crowded with coolies and mandarins, but it was by far the greater city. Yang might have been walking through a mud village for all the attention he paid.

He stopped in front of the hotel, looking left and right and then upwards. "The sky is good," was all he said.

I looked up, too. The sky was almost clear with faint ripples of high cloud that put me in mind of fish bones.

The reception desk sat between two potted palms. A spotty young man with a starched collar stood behind it. I took charge of the checking in, not that there was any need. Mr Yang's English was certainly up to scratch, and he understood the procedure. There was, however, a problem.

"Animals are not permitted in the rooms," the desk clerk said, seeing the cat in its wicker basket. The collar gave him a lofty air. He did not approve of either Mr Yang or me.

"An exception may be made in this instance," I said. "The room was booked by Mr Arthur Renville. Mr Yang is his honoured guest."

"I don't know Arthur Renville from Adam," said the clerk. "Animals are not permitted in the rooms."

"I had better speak to the manager then," I said rather

warmly. The manager would certainly know Arthur, and he would put the clerk right.

"There is no need," said Mr Yang.

"Animals are not permitted," repeated the clerk.

Mr Yang looked coolly at him. The clerk turned his back, pretending to be reading entries in a ledger. Yang's eyes were still fixed on him.

"It's no use your standing there," the clerk said without looking round. "It's in the hotel rules. You'll have to find somewhere else or leave that thing outside."

The seconds passed like treacle dripping. I wanted to call for the manager, but Yang raised a hand to halt me, still looking at the back of the clerk's head. I swear the cat was looking at the clerk, too. The man fingered his stiff collar unconsciously. I was about to repeat my request to talk to the manager when the clerk turned around.

"Very well then, I suppose." He opened the register without looking at Mr Yang. "Of course, there will be an additional charge for your… animal."

"Of course." Mr Yang did not take the pen but left me to fill in the register. As I wrote out the details, his hand rested on the desk, and I noted one oddity about his manicure. The nails were perfect, except the nail on his little finger, which was long and curved as a talon, extending past the end of his ring finger.

The bellboy had been riveted throughout the performance. He kept looking from Yang to me and back as he escorted us to a room and stood in the doorway.

The Tulse Hill Hotel is your typical railway hotel, the same as the rest of them up and down the country. These places are occupied mainly by commercial travellers and incline towards the functional. Many of the rooms are little more than hutches for single men kept away from home by their business, an unhappy breed who sit on wooden chairs at the regulation writing desks, adding up their sales for the day or arranging their samples.

This was one of the better rooms. It was a good size with a high ceiling and a sense of open space. There was a bay window, blue-and-white-striped wallpaper, and a thick carpet underfoot.

The bed and the armchairs looked comfortable enough.

"It's a good room," I assured Yang. He nodded slightly. I tossed the gawping bellboy a tanner, which he snatched with one hand, and sent him off before arranging Yang's luggage.

Yang remained in place, as motionless as he had been in the station. I wanted to suggest his calling for a cup of tea and relaxing for a bit but was uncertain how to comport myself. The cat, a big tabby, stirred in its basket and uttered a low sound.

Yang looked at his wristwatch, a fine square Dunhill—or a Chinese copy of one. "It will be convenient for you to meet me in the lobby at nine o'clock tomorrow morning, Mr Stubbs." His tone indicated that this was an order.

"That will be quite convenient, sir."

"And Mr Stubbs, it is not customary for Europeans to call Chinese 'sir.'"

"I never knew that. How should I address you properly?"

He seemed puzzled at the question. "It does not matter," he said after a minute. I could not tell whether he was appeased or offended. "Tomorrow at nine o'clock."

"Thank you." I left him standing in the hotel room, immobile as a statue. Yang gave nothing away except what he wished. He would not relax, if he ever did, until I was gone.

Chapter Three

A Tour of Norwood

There was a fine motorcar outside the hotel the next morning, a black six-cylinder Daimler, fresh from the showroom, waxed and polished to a shine. I paused to admire it a moment before going inside and finding a new clerk at the desk.

"Mr Stubbs, isn't it? I believe we have a mutual acquaintance in Mr Renville." His name was Walker, and he gave a wink to signify we were both on the same job of watching Yang. "There's a gentleman from the motor-rental company waiting over there who needs you to sign some papers."

The rental agent asked if Mr Yang would be requiring a chauffeur. I don't drive myself, but I could think of a dozen of Arthur's circle who would take on the job, so I sent the agent on his way.

Yang appeared at nine o'clock on the dot, dressed in an off-white suit no less smart than his previous outfit. I mentioned the matter of the chauffeur.

"We do not need a driver. I will drive; you will provide navigation." Yang passed me an odd piece of thick brown paper, about three inches square. There was an address in block letters on one side and Chinese writing on the other. "You know this place?"

"Certainly. It's over the other side of Dulwich."

We sat in the car, which smelled of fresh leather and oiled wood, while Yang familiarised himself with the controls. He lightly touched the handles and levers in turn and stroked the steering wheel. I did not dare to offer help, and when Yang pushed the starter button, the powerful engine roared to life.

"It's a good car," I said.

"I drive a Daimler in Shanghai," said Yang, flicking the indicator. "Now, what direction?"

Yang drove well, coping with the busy traffic without difficulty. I had imagined Shanghai as a place of rickshaws and oxcarts and carriages but began to think that I may have been mistaken. I resolved to ask Reg about it.

I found the address easily enough even though it was out of the way. The road was a rutted lane, and the house stood by itself, almost concealed in the trees and surrounded by an overgrown garden. It was a ramshackle construction, built in several stages over a long period. It looked at least half-derelict. The roof slates were askew, but the windows were intact. A thin stream of smoke rose from the chimney.

Yang indicated for me to remain in the car. He crossed the road and knocked on the door. We waited for a good three minutes. I saw a face at an upstairs window. It appeared so briefly that I couldn't tell whether it was a man or a woman. Nobody answered the door. At length, Yang came back across the muddy road and, taking out a silver fountain pen and business card, used the bonnet of the car for a writing table. He was close enough for me to see that he did not write but just drew a simple, looping design. Then he posted it in the letterbox.

As he stepped back into the car, I noted that, except for the soles of his shoes, there was not one speck of mud on him. He walked with the grace of a cat, treading lightly. Heel and toe touched at the same moment, as though Yang had been trained to walk silently and did it without thinking.

"We will return here later." Yang passed me another slip with an address on it. "Here is the next address."

"Certainly, but this lane's a dead end. You'll have to drive in reverse the way we came."

Instead, Yang turned the wheel sharply, going forward and then back, changing the heavy gears with little effort. In a few seconds, he'd turned the big Daimler around in less space than I would have thought possible. Yang was not a man whom you could tell what to do.

"Which direction next?" he asked as he started back down the lane.

The second address was a very different affair. This was a comfortable suburban villa near Crown Point, set on a street with a dozen other buildings like it. There was nothing to distinguish the house except for a discreet wooden notice board next to the garden gate.

"'Upper Norwood Theosophist Circle,'" I read.

"That is correct. Please remain here."

I watched again as Yang went and knocked on the door. This time, a maid answered his knock. A minute later, a grey-haired man came to the door, and he and Yang conversed for a few minutes. I strained to read any of the messages posted on the board and wondered what a Theosophist Circle was.

"We will return here in a few days," Yang announced as he opened the car door. "I have been invited to attend a séance."

"What, calling up spirits and table rapping and all that?"

"I believe so."

"I understand you're here on a religious mission," I offered. Reg would be pleased, I thought. It was not a direct question but close enough to the point.

"Indeed," said Yang. "My purpose is not unconnected with the Theosophist Circle."

"I'd love to see one of those séances for myself," I said without really thinking. "You see them on the stage and in the pictures, but a real séance must be something else."

Yang hesitated for the smallest fraction of a second. And yet, in hindsight, I believe that in that moment he conceived an entirely new plan of action, one that included me as an accomplice. He had weighed me up, judging my strengths and weaknesses, what sort of tool I would make, and how I could be used. And he put his plan into effect.

"You will attend, also. It will be more convenient for you not to be associated with me at this point, you understand."

I did not understand at all, but I pretended that I did. "Certainly. I suppose you have attended many of these occasions in Shanghai?"

"Never," he said. "I will now inspect this area on foot. Direct me to a parking space for the Daimler."

I guided him to the dairy yard, which had plenty of room outside. With no deliveries due until the next morning, they would not mind us parking there. I had Yang wait a minute while I collared a small boy to act as a guardian. It would not do for such a fine vehicle to be molested.

Yang set off in a circuit with the Theosophist house roughly in the middle. It was a reconnaissance, but of what sort I found it hard to say. He seemed to give equal weight to everything; the buildings, the trees, the clouds all seemed to attract his attention in turn. I tried to see the place as he was seeing it, but there was nothing worthy of attention as far as I could tell. Except for the two of us, of course—the small Chinese gentleman in white with his oversized English guide in black.

We attracted curious looks from passers-by. If Yang had been dressed more quietly, he would not have attracted attention, but his fancy suit, multiplied by his being Chinese, set minds to working and tongues wagging. Fortunately, we did not encounter any groups of schoolboys, who would not have let such a peculiar pair pass without loud comment and perhaps some experimenting on the effect of throwing mud at that immaculate suit.

We stopped by the Great Pond on Beulah Hill while Yang took a cigarette from a slim silver case and fitted it to an amber holder. Instead of matches, he had a silver lighter with the same Oriental pattern as the case, and lit up with a single flick.

"A pond at the top of a hill is unusual," said Yang.

"I believe the cattlemen used to water their herds here when they brought them to market." This information came from my father, learned from his father who remembered when cattle were driven into Norwood from the fields of Surrey.

"How does the pond remain full? No streams feed it here on the hill."

"Perhaps there's a spring. There's lots of underground water… the old Beulah Spa is just up the road there."

Yang shook his head fractionally but said nothing. He took out an old copper coin with a square hole punched through it, held in his palm a second, and then tossed the coin, spinning, into the water. Yang watched the ripples as if reading words on the water, and only when they had faded to nothing did he set off again.

We stopped again outside the gates of the vast, brick-built blocks of the Home and Hospital for Incurables. Yang looked the structure up and down as though he was thinking of buying it. I told him how it was a hospital for people with a chronic sickness such as consumption and palsy or for unfortunates who had been born deformed and the like. And because it said 1894 on the wall, I could tell him when it was built.

"Why is it here?"

"Well." I scratched my chin. "I suppose it's because it's such a healthy locality. Up here on the hill, out of the smoke of the city and all that. No pea soupers here."

"Indeed." Yang stood politely aside as two nurses pushed patients in wheelchairs past us. One of the patients stared at him rather rudely from his chair but looked away as soon as Yang returned his gaze. "Many people have died here," Yang observed. I shrugged. We moved on.

We stopped again at the bottom of Crown Dale, where Yang cocked his head and seemed to listen. Big crows were hopping around in the park opposite, and I wondered if he was eavesdropping on them, but he moved on without comment.

Nothing seemed to quite please him. It was as though England was lacking some important quality that he'd expected to find.

Close to the summit of Central Hill, Yang took out a paper packet and extracted a pinch of white powder, which he tossed into the air. A delivery boy pushing his bicycle up the hill stopped to look while Yang repeated the gesture before replacing the packet in an inner pocket.

Yang was obviously amused by my perplexity, which seemed to cheer him no end. "In English, you call it geomancy."

I didn't call anything "geomancy" and doubted that was even an English word.

"We study the movement of wind and water and the more subtle currents that affect human life."

"Oh, I see," I said.

Yang smoothed his goatee with one hand. "It is a superstition. We Chinese are a very superstitious people, after all."

"I would never suggest such a thing. As for subtle currents—well, I saw how you stared down that hotel clerk."

"Ah, you think I have hypnotic skills?" He sounded amused. "All petty officials like to show their power. I did not contest with the clerk. I gave him the freedom to show he could use his power by denying me the room. Then, I allowed him to consider the consequences of his actions. Like all petty officials, he preferred to concede rather than be overruled by his superior later."

I recalled what Reg had said about the importance of not losing face. Perhaps it was not an exclusively Chinese concern.

"We say 'To control a horse, you put it in a large field,'" said Yang.

"Is that a saying of Confucius?"

Yang laughed, a double bark. "Ha! Ha! It is a saying of the sage Lao-Tzu."

I was pleased that he was finally talking but stumped on how to carry on the conversation. I ploughed on with the first thing that occurred to me. "I don't know much about Chinese philosophy. But you know what does interest me? The Fists of Harmony, the Boxers. They can break a brick with one punch, using mental energy. My friend saw one of them at a Chinese Circus. Bang, bang, bang, bricks broken right in half, one after the other. I'd like to know how they do that."

Yang walked on several paces in silence. "The Boxers," he said at last. "The Boxers thought their magic would protect them against the Westerners' bullets. It failed. They thoughts spirits would aid them. They did not. China is still paying reparations for the Boxer Rebellion after thirty years. Four hundred million pieces of silver."

"I didn't mean—"

Yang's raised hand silenced me, the curved fingernail before my face. "It is more profitable to study guns than magic Fists of Righteous Harmony."

"I'm a boxer myself," I said, trying to explain. "I mean, a pugilist, you know." I mimed a boxing stance. "That's the only reason I'm interested."

"Indeed," he said.

It seemed I had touched a raw nerve. To get away from the subject and to fill the silence, again I seized on the first thing that came into my mind. "Sometimes bullets don't work, as a matter of fact." I told him the story about the shooting outside the pub and how Collins had emptied his pistol without any effect. It was the most exciting thing that had happened recently, and people were still talking about it. "Have you ever heard anything like it?"

"Hah. An English ghost story" was all Yang would say.

We walked on until the towers of the Crystal Palace came in sight, followed by the majestic building itself. That did impress him and rightly so; there was nothing like it in the world. But he seemed to appreciate the siting more than the majestic structure itself.

We talked little during the rest of the perambulation. We stopped at the bottom of Gypsy Hill, and he asked about the grassy space. From somewhere in my memory, I dredged up that it had been a plague pit, which seemed to satisfy him.

Writing it down now, I see how few words Yang actually spoke. Yet I felt that I was starting to understand him a little.

It was difficult to explain this to Arthur as he cross-questioned me in the Hollybush Public House that evening. It was late, but Arthur's working day had only just begun, and we were interrupted by a steady stream of messengers and telephone calls, relayed from the bar. There was a consignment to be disposed of, and it had to be done quickly.

Arthur was at least satisfied that I was doing my job and had established some rapport with Yang. Reg was on hand to provide advice on Chinese matters, but Arthur was more concerned with the English people whom Yang had contacted.

"Spiritualists," said Arthur. "That's a rum business. Plenty of room for trickery and relieving folk of their money. Or he may only be going there to put you off the scent. If he invited you to join in, it can't be secret."

"What about that house the other side of Dulwich though?"

"Oh, that's old Willie Whatley's house," said Arthur as though it was common knowledge. "They're an odd breed, the

Whatleys—part Gypsy. His father was a fortune-teller, years ago, and a horse doctor, quite well-known. There's only Whatley and his daughter left. He still sells a few charms to old women."

"What does Yang want with them?"

"We'll find out. We've got pretty close tabs on Mr Yang. I can tell you every piece of post he's received, the visitors he's had at the hotel, what he's been eating."

"Really?" I could not believe that Arthur would really have this level of surveillance.

"Plain boiled rice and boiled chicken, I am reliably informed." Arthur patted my arm. "You're just one cog in this observational apparatus, Stubbsy."

"I wonder if he's brought the cat to eat," said Reg thoughtfully. "They do that, you know, in South China."

"My information is that he requested fish for the cat," said Arthur. "And left strict instructions about it not being disturbed by the chambermaids. He talks to it in Chinese. Also, he lets it out at night. I don't believe that cat is on the menu. Probably has it to keep the English mice from nesting in his expensive handkerchiefs."

"It's not civilised, is it, taking an animal into an hotel?" Reg muttered.

"You often see ladies in these hotels with their little Pekingese," I said. "If a Chinese dog, why not a Chinese cat?"

"That's different," said Reg. "Also, one thing I should warn you about, Harry. I hear you carried Yang's luggage yesterday."

"What of it?"

"In the Middle Kingdom, servants don't carry luggage. It's degrading. They always get a street porter to carry things. Yang must think you're very low." He seemed to find this amusing.

"You might have mentioned that before," said Arthur. "But I want to know what he's doing here. What is it he's looking for?"

I tried to explain to them how Yang's survey had made me feel uncomfortable. It was like when the dentist used that sharp probe, poking around to find tender spots. Yang was looking for tender spots in our neighbourhood. I remembered how Reg had described Chinese doctors sticking pins in people. I wondered if Yang had something like that in mind.

"What's geomancy?"

"It's just something they do," said Reg. "Yang is a Fang-Shi, or pretending to be one—a sort of Taoist magician. Taoism is a hodgepodge of folklore and superstition. These Fang-Shi go about selling mineral potions and horoscopes to people who believe in that sort of thing."

"Why did he get hot under the collar when I mentioned the Boxers?"

"Did you?" Reg gave a low chuckle. "You shouldn't have brought that up! That whole rebellion was stirred up by Taoist priests. They don't like *foreign devils* being in China."

"Can they really break bricks...?"

"Of course not," said Reg. "It's just a trick. Breaking a brick with your hand is a physical impossibility. You, of all people, ought to know that."

I tried to explain how Yang was moving on a plane of his own. He was not seeing the Norwood that I knew but another place, where there were spiritualist circles and fortune-tellers. He was looking at the subtle currents of wind and water.

I had a shrewd idea that there was more to the pond on Beulah Hill, and perhaps the Home and Hospital for Incurables, than met the eye. Yang was on a religious mission, or a superstitious one. This was not any ordinary business to do with opium dens and gangsters; of that I was sure—even though Yang looked somewhat like a gangster himself. His suit was not so well cut that I had failed to spot the automatic pistol tucked into the side of his belt.

Chapter Four

The Séance

The days followed a pattern. Each day, Yang would have a timetable of appointments that we would drive to, or I would be called on to guide him in a walking tour. We visited the Crystal Palace three times, inside and out. I mentioned the National Cat Show there, but he would not be drawn out on the subject of cats. Our perambulations took in West Norwood Cemetery and the lakes.

Yang often spent afternoons in his room. One day, when the rain was unremitting and forecast to stay that way, he sent me away as soon as I turned up in the morning. He did not like English rain.

Our walks were interrupted by queer little rituals. He sometimes stopped by a building and asked me to explain it. Once, he sat down cross-legged on a flagstone, having dusted it clean with his handkerchief, and took out a little bundle of twigs no bigger than matchsticks. He divided them into two piles and started counting them off by fours. Having completed the calculation, he repeated the process of combining, dividing, and counting by fours several times.

A woman with a shopping basket stopped to ask me what the Chinese gentleman was doing.

"I believe it is known as geomancy," I said. "It's an ancient Chinese art of divination."

"Oh," she said, not approvingly.

On other occasions, Yang took out a small brass pendulum and gravely observed its motion without comment, or ignited a cone of rice paper with his lighter and watched it rise into the air like a balloon before it dissolved into fine ash. He did not comment on the results of these operations, and his face betrayed nothing.

He was also given to occasional bouts of philosophy. Once a butterfly alighted on Yang's sleeve, confused perhaps by the half inch of bright yellow shirt cuff. For a moment I thought he might grab the insect, but he watched until it flew off.

"Once I dreamed I was a butterfly," he said meditatively. "When I woke I did not know if I was a man who had dreamed I was a butterfly, or a butterfly dreaming I was a man."

This sounded very much like a literary quotation. I was lost for a reply, until I was rescued by the Immortal Bard. And my English teacher, who beat the words into me.

"'We are such stuff as dreams are made on,'" I said. "'Our little life is rounded with a sleep.'"

"Indeed," said Yang.

For my part, I tagged along and answered what questions he had. Years of making deliveries on a bicycle had given me a pretty fair knowledge of the geography of the neighbourhood, though in the field of history I am somewhat deficient.

I made efforts not to look too shabby. I could not match Yang's standards of appearance, but I bought some fresh collars and new ties and took extra care with my shaving and grooming.

Once, as we drove past my father's shop, Yang asked sharply, "That shop is important to you?"

The sign read Stubbs Family Butchers as clear as day. Yang could hardly have failed to make a connection with the names. But I am not ashamed of what I am. I have never pretended to be anything more than the son of a butcher.

"This is my father's shop. My family has been here for generations."

"So, a butcher." Yang considered this. "Does your father chop meat with a cleaver?"

"That is part and parcel of the trade, yes."

"How often does he replace the cleaver?"

"Never," I said, well remembering the big, square-bladed chopper moving briskly up and down over a carcass. "A good butcher never damages the blade by trying to slice through bone. He cuts through the joints, and the cleaver never wears out. My father has had the same one for years."

"Indeed!" Yang said, nodding briskly. "The same in China. Your father is a wise man! Many ministers are not so wise!"

I could not detect mockery in his tone. Yang seemed as impressed as if my father had been a general or a bank manager. I do not know why a butcher who cut meat should be revered. It must have been another peculiarity of the Chinese view of things.

One day, Yang produced a slip of paper with Captain Hall's address and said that he would visit the Captain to convey his uncle's good wishes. I mentioned to Yang that it was normal practice, in England, to give notice before a visit and that perhaps it would be in order to send a note first.

Yang smoothed his beard with one hand. "Indeed." He drove on.

From my viewpoint, sitting in the car, I saw Mrs Hall open the door and her look of surprise and dismay at the well-dressed Chinese gentleman on her doorstep. Afterwards, I could see Yang clearly in the Hall's front room. He was standing with his back to the window and had not taken off his hat or his coat. It did not look like an especially comfortable or relaxed encounter for the Halls.

Yang emerged again after a few minutes with a face stonier than ever. The Halls closed the door quickly behind him. I learned later from Arthur that Yang had stalked in and started making comments about Hall's health that sounded like veiled threats. However, before Yang had gotten very far, the parrot started screeching at him in Mandarin. That old parrot was a character; he was as travelled as Captain Hall and well-known for his powers of swearing in many languages. Something he said drove Yang off sharpish, to Captain Hall's great relief.

A second visit to Whatley was no more successful. This time, Yang stayed in the car and sent me to knock on the door. To my surprise, a woman opened it, looking at me through an opening only as wide as the chain would allow.

"There's nothing for you here." She was in a dirty housecoat;

hair fell lankly about her shoulders, framing an unhealthy, pale complexion. "We can't help him find what he's looking for."

"Mr Yang would like to talk with Mr Whatley, please," I said.

She raised a hand in a defensive gesture as though she thought I would spit at her. "We don't talk with the likes of him." She shut the door. I heard a key rattle and bolts being shot.

I conveyed this to Yang, who merely nodded. Nothing seemed to surprise him.

Not long afterwards, on Yang's instruction, I parked the car a quarter mile from the Theosophist Circle. Yang went first, and I followed ten minutes afterwards. I checked the notice board in the garden and confirmed the time of the séance and that it was open to all. The Circle encouraged visitors to come and see for themselves, being a church like any other and always eager to increase the congregation.

The maid took my coat and hat and directed me to the crowded sitting room, where a dozen people were already gathered. The hostess greeted me at once. I had always been self-conscious in these situations, and with half an ear missing after recent events, I felt even more freakish in polite company.

She was a lady of advanced years. From a distance, her bobbed auburn hair led to some confusion about her age, but I soon concluded that it was a wig.

"Everything's on first-name terms here," she told me and insisted that I call her Lavinia. The clothes hung loosely on her fleshless limbs, but she carried her years lightly and was quick and sharp as a bird for all that. She wore an amethyst necklace and a great many rings and bangles, and she turned about rapidly like a hen looking over her brood.

Lavinia was a widow. For some years, her passion had been gardening, but she had been forced to give it up on account of rheumatism. She had moved away from her big house with the big garden, which she could no longer bear to look at, and bought Maycot. The place had, for some reason, revived her interest in spiritualism, which she had toyed with forty years previously.

"Ours is a pure Theosophy," she told me. "Not the debased

nonsense of that Blavatsky woman. We are, I should say, Paracelsian. You know Paracelsus?"

"Only from Mr Robert Browning's work." I had greatly enjoyed his epic poem *Paracelsus*, about the old alchemist's quest for truth, though some passages were a little disturbing. "I believe it was written near here, by a curious coincidence."

"There are no coincidences," she told me gravely. "Excuse me, I have to attend a rather special guest. Do have yourself a cup of tea. And you'll want to read this." She pushed a pamphlet entitled *What Is Theosophy?* into my hands and was gone.

I pretended to read the pamphlet while looking around the room. It was a decent place though somewhat spoiled by some ill-advised artwork of the primitive school. I suspected the paintings were by some local amateur and represented theosophical themes. The reproduction furniture was of good quality, and the carpet was plush beneath my feet. Above me, the chandelier—a garish affair with a thousand scales of purple glass—spoke of money.

Mr Yang was the special guest that Lavinia was attending to, aided by a plump young woman and a man with wispy hair whose back was to me. These were the bigwigs, I decided. The others were all over sixty, the majority of them women, standing in pairs or threesomes with little animation. While I was evaluating them and realising how I stood out, a tall, elderly gentlemen in tweeds took me by the elbow.

"Harry, isn't it?" he said. "I'm Victor."

I thought he was a retired military man, though he had actually been in the Indian Civil Service for many years and had retired as provincial governor somewhere in Uttar Pradesh, which, if you are unfamiliar with Indian geography, is near the Himalayan Mountains. His manner was one of forced cordiality. "Can I just have a small word with you?"

I found myself in the kitchen, backed against the wall, with Victor bearing down on me. The maid hastily piled teacups on the tray and fled the room.

"I like to think I'm a pretty fair judge of character," Victor said, coming directly to the point. "We don't see too many new faces around here. Those we get are seeking consolation and wishing to contact a departed one, or sometimes we get someone who's just come to gawk and scoff. But I don't think you're a grieving relative or a scoffer. You look very much like a bailiff's man to me. What the devil are you doing here?"

I swallowed, taken aback by his tone. Victor was tall, and he carried himself with considerable authority. His gaze was as intimidating as a magistrate's. He had spent years dealing with petitioners in India and was inured to soft-soaping and wheedling.

I hesitated.

"Out with it, man," Victor snapped.

For one moment, the idea of making a run for it flashed into my mind. My lips were moving, though, even before I knew what I was going to say. I did not stop to think through the tangled situation or consider telling him about Yang and Arthur Renville.

"I've always been a down-to-earth sort," I started. "I've paid more attention to the football results than the great questions of the human soul. But lately, I've seen some things that have made me wonder about everything."

"Have you indeed," Victor said with heavy emphasis on the last word.

I did not know where to start or what to say about what I had witnessed in the Shackleton affair. I'm sure my confusion showed. Victor's eyes bored into me.

"Look." I opened my shirt and drew out a fine chain. On it hung the ring that was too dainty for my sausage fingers, the ring set with a five-pointed green stone.

Victor's expression changed from hostility to baffled wonderment as he held the ring in the light and examined it. "Good Lord! It's real… do you know what this is? Where did you get it?"

"The story is quite a convoluted one. The ring did not come without a price."

"I've only seen one like it once before," he said, fascinated by the stone. "It was on the hand of an old Swami I met in curious circumstances…"

"I should be happy to tell you about it on another occasion."

"I should like to hear that story very much," he said, looking at me with new appreciation. Evidently, the ring was enough to persuade him that my intentions were honest. "I bet that story is a corker. Well, well, well. Nothing personal, Harry, but we don't often meet fellow seekers. I'm afraid I was rattled by something else and... anyway, we'd better get back to the throng."

We returned to the sitting room, where a cup of tea was pressed into my hand, and with Victor, I joined a group that included Lavinia and Yang.

"I used to take an interest in gardening," Lavinia was telling Yang. "And this is much the same, you know. A garden must be nurtured to reach its potential, not allowed to run riot. Theosophy must be guided towards its goal of uniting esoteric wisdom of every type with science. Left alone, it degenerates into a jungle."

"Madame Blavatsky," added Victor, "our illustrious standard-bearer and former occupant of this house, was a bit of a one for those kinds of weeds. To be fair, she did bring the Vedas to the attention of the West, but—"

"That woman did no end of harm to Theosophy," said Lavinia. "She knew nothing of science and precious little of the esoteric. She commandeered Theosophy and sailed it away from its true ends."

"Quite so," Victor conceded.

"'The wisest woman in Europe,' indeed," she fumed. I had a feeling this was a discussion they had had many times before and were planning on enacting again.

"I rather think T. S. Eliot was making fun of her," said Victor, looking around for support. "You know *The Waste Land*?"

Neither Yang nor I was familiar with that work, so the subject lapsed.

"Anyway, like a garden that has been left untended, our little circle needed pruning—there were a few members who had to be encouraged to leave. And it needed new growth, like Elizabeth, our Mediator, and Victor, who you might say is a transplant, who are both experienced in the Indian Vedic tradition."

"And Howard," said Victor.

"A prize bloom," said Lavinia, "if you don't mind the expression."

Howard shrugged casually.

"He's got more original scholarship in his little finger than the rest of us put together," said Victor. "He's the greatest expert on Palingenesis in England—he's written two monographs so far, and we're pressing him for a third."

"I am not familiar with this word," said Yang.

Victor shied slightly when Yang turned to him. He was ill at ease with the Chinese visitor.

"A form of alchemy," said Lavinia. "I'm sure there's a Chinese word for it."

"Few people have heard of Palingenesis," said Howard dryly. He was a pudgy, anaemic young man with wispy, receding hair and steel-rimmed spectacles. "It is the art of recovering the form of a thing from its ashes."

"Show him the pictures," urged Victor.

"This is one of my experiments," Howard said. He drew a set of photographs wrapped in wax paper from an inner pocket and passed them to Yang. "The first picture shows a test tube containing salts extracted from the ashes of a rose. In the second, heat is applied to the test tube, and you can see the results."

Yang examined each photograph in the sequence. "Shoots grow from the ashes, then buds and leaves and a flower. Your rose, no doubt."

"Lavinia found a young man to do the photography," said Victor. "I believe these pictures are unique."

"The phoenix, which is resurrected from its ashes, is also part of Eastern legend as it is in the West, is it not?" asked Lavinia.

"Indeed." Yang frowned slightly, an expression so unusual that it looked theatrical. He smoothed his beard. "To me, this resembled the occasion when the sage encountered a hermit living by a river. The hermit explained that after meditating for twenty years, he was able to walk across the water. The sage said 'Poor fellow! Did you not know there is a ferry, just around the river bend, that will take you across for a farthing?'"

The company laughed awkwardly.

"There are many flower stalls in London," Yang added.

"It's more about the principle of the thing—"

"You're quite right, Mr Yang. It's not that remarkable," said Howard, cutting Victor off. "After all, Browne did it two hundred years ago. Palingenesis was performed in front of the Royal Society last century—Phillips reproduced a sparrow from its ashes. Even Yeats did it—WB Yeats, the Irish poet. He described his experiments to Madame Blavatsky in this very room. And, as you can see from the sixth and seventh pictures, as soon as the heat is removed, the phantom crumbles back into dust. It is insubstantial, vastly inferior to the cheapest flower-stall bloom."

"But it's a phenomenon that might explain much. Robert Boyle suggested it might explain the Resurrection. Of, ah, Jesus, you know." Victor added to Yang. "Or apparitions of the dead in graveyards, rising from their dust."

"It's only a theory," interjected Elizabeth.

"But you see," said Victor, "Howard has been experimenting with fixing the phantom with radium salts as one fixes a photograph."

"Merely a hypothesis as Elizabeth says," Howard said carelessly. "I shall write up my experiments, such as they are, one day."

"I think it's delightful to call up flowers from ash," said Lavinia. "One day, I may be able to carry a whole garden around with me in a case and produce bouquets whenever I like. What is more important is that it gives proof positive that science and esoteric wisdom can be fruitful together. Proof positive that is portable. I am afraid we have twisted poor Howard's arm..."

"We persuaded him to send samples to an American gentleman," said Victor. "A wealthy New Englander who's absolutely crazy about European magic."

"Think what we could do with his sponsorship!" Lavinia beamed at Howard.

"Please excuse my poor ignorance," said Yang. "Why has this been neglected by Western scientists?"

"They can't make it work because they don't know the words," said Howard.

"But it is scientific," said Victor quickly. "Howard can tell you all about it. I understand while he's explaining it—it's all to do with 'entropy not enthalpy' of heat—but five minutes later, it's out of my head. Tell our visitor about thermodynamics."

"Please do," said Lavinia. The two were like parents coaxing a shy child to perform in front of strangers.

"I don't think we want to go into that now," said Howard, adjusting his glasses. This was not enough for his audience, and he was forced to go on. He gave a slight smile. "As with many things—metallurgy, crop rotation—the ancients stumbled on the technique without understanding how it works. You know, there was a place in Spain that made excellent swords using a secret, magical recipe. The smiths used to hold the iron in the fire while reciting a certain psalm three times. Of course, what they didn't realise was that it was the exact timing that this gave them, and not the words themselves, that was important in forming the metal to the perfect balance between hardness and flexibility. Or at least, that's how science interprets it. But it might be the harmonic vibrations of the voice, or perhaps even the information contained in the words – there's so much we do not know."

"Only Palingenesis, it's about reversing time—and organising principles—" Lavinia prompted. "Paracelsus says it's like magnetism…"

"I'm simply picking away at the science behind an established phenomenon, isolating the active ingredient, like extracting quinine from the bark of the fever tree." Howard stopped and looked down. That was all we were going to get of science.

"Most interesting," said Yang with the slightest of bows.

"The boy is too modest," said Victor. "Hides his light under a bushel."

"A little nurturing will see his talent flourish," said Lavinia. "Now Elizabeth, my dear, are you quite ready to face the Otherworld?"

Elizabeth had been stifling a yawn, bored by this technical version of Theosophy. She was waiting for her moment to shine.

"Quite ready, thank you, Lavinia. I do not think the Spirits will disappoint this afternoon."

"With Mr Yang's powers added to our own, the effects should be wonderful," said Lavinia.

At a nod from Lavinia, Victor rearranged the furniture with the help of some others. I was directed to move some chairs; it was all very democratic.

"We are privileged today to be joined by a distinguished visitor from China, an adept in the ways of Taoism," Lavinia told the assembled company while Yang gazed blandly into the distance. She went on to explain how we owe gunpowder to the Taoist alchemists, and what other things they had discovered while Europe was lost in the Dark Ages.

Elizabeth took her place at a circular table, flanked by Lavinia and Victor with Yang and Howard completing the circle, while the rest of us looked on from a row of folding chairs. Instead of just touching fingers, the five sitters joined hands—"to make a better connection," Lavinia explained. Holding hands with Yang and touching that long fingernail might have been disconcerting, but Howard gave no sign of noticing.

The thick velvet curtains were drawn, and the darkness of the room was relieved only by a small metal lantern in the centre of the table, which cast a low, flickering light over the proceedings. All you could make out were the faces of the sitters.

The transformation was total. In just two minutes, an ordinary suburban drawing room had taken on the aspect of a temple crypt where some ancient ceremony was to be enacted. First, Lavinia spoke a prayer—or invocation as she termed it—in a language that I did not recognise. Then Victor uttered his own brief incantation in a high-pitched, wailing voice.

An expectant hush fell over the room. My senses were sharpened, on the alert for trickery or stage magic.

"I am listening." Elizabeth's round white face was oddly distinct in the candlelight. "I am listening."

The silence stretched on for a minute, two minutes. My eyes adjusted to the darkness. I could make out the pale outlines of the curtains, the rounded forms of the people around me.

"I am Flavia, wife of the governor of Londinium," said Elizabeth. She sounded too much like a railway-station announcer for me to be impressed. Questions crowded my mind about how she could be speaking in English and why she still said Londinium rather than plain London.

"Greetings once more, sister Flavia," said Lavinia. "We honour you, who are our gatekeeper to the Otherworld, our guide through the tracks of eternity."

"Is that you, sister Lavinia? I salute you from beyond the veil."

"Have you others there with you? May we speak with the one from far Atlantis who you promised us before?"

"You may," said Elizabeth gravely. "Let it be known that I keep my vow."

It was too preposterous. They wanted us to believe that contacting the afterlife was like getting the girl at the switchboard to put you through to a local number. I'm as open-minded as the next man, but that performance strained my credulity.

"Gah." Elizabeth grunted the sound in an impossibly low voice. She lowered her eyes and started breathing deeply then began a low mutter of harsh, jagged syllables. It sounded like some simple, made-up language with many repetitions.

"Who is there?" asked Lavinia.

Elizabeth's voice doubled up on itself by some trick of ventriloquism so that there were two voices speaking, and then many, a whole crowd of them muttering the same rhythmic phrase over and over.

"Tell us who you are," said Victor.

Elizabeth's mouth seemed to be moving independently of the sound, which made me wonder about concealed gramophone players. And then she gave a deep belch—which under other circumstances might have reduced an audience to laughter—before continuing her low gabble.

It was less of an entertainment than I expected. I thought the séance was all about contacting people one knew to talk to them on the other side. Or at least, you might speak to known historical personages. Julius Caesar might tell you where his crown was buried or something, but this was all meaningless.

I yawned, and the candlelight flickered and grew dimmer. The shadows across Elizabeth's features wavered, and for a moment, it seemed that she had no face at all. She started rocking backwards and forwards, chanting louder.

"What is she saying?" asked Yang.

"In the name of Tau-Tri-Delta," said Victor. "I abjure you to speak your name."

Elizabeth gave a convulsive jerk as though she was being sick. At first, I thought she really was sick, but what came out of her mouth was not vomit but a peculiar greyish substance. The only thing I could compare it to would be frogspawn ejected underwater by the female frog: billowing, gelatinous stuff, and lumpy, but with no real substance. Except that this was alive, stretching and easing itself into a snake that reached halfway across the table before rearing up slowly and dissolving in the air.

"Stop it," said Lavinia.

Elizabeth twitched again, and this time, a double stream of ectoplasm rolled out, uncoiling and reaching like a pair of serpents or tentacles. It looked, frankly, quite menacing, and Yang leaned back in his seat away from it. Seemingly, he could not, or would not, let go of the hands of the other two.

The ectoplasm fell apart again into a smoky slush that dribbled off the table in all directions and disintegrated into nothingness. Already, a third and greater wave was coming. Elizabeth's jaws were opened wider than I would have thought possible, as though they were being forced apart from inside, but still she was gargling that low, rhythmic chant.

"Break the circle!" Victor was calm and forceful, but there was urgency in his voice.

"I can't!" said Howard.

All the sitters all started talking together in a chaotic babble. Like a man who accidentally takes hold of a high-voltage cable and finds himself unable to let go, the sitters were locked together. The ectoplasm surged out into a great puddle that flexed itself, a grey snail emerging from its shell, sliding forwards, and dividing into triple streams that each wriggled toward Yang.

"Stop it! Stop it!" Lavinia's howl was clearly audible above the hubbub.

There was consternation among those in the audience.

Clearly, this was not a regular part of the séance. I hesitated then stood up. Taking hold of someone being electrocuted is a dangerous thing to do. The sitters had more experience—more psychic resilience—than me; the force that ran through them might burn out my nerves. There seemed little alternative though.

Yang had quietly pushed himself back as far as he could go. A grey cobra reared up before him, taking on definition and form like a magic-lantern picture gradually coming into focus. I took Yang's wrist in one hand and Victor's in the other and tried to pull them apart. It was more difficult than I expected. A grey form was writhing and splitting in the corner of my eye. I gave a sharp wrench and pulled their hands apart.

The room went dark, and the chanting halted as suddenly and completely as though Elizabeth had been struck with a hammer. There was a moment of silence before the turmoil erupted.

Someone had the presence of mind to turn on the electric light. Elizabeth was slumped forwards, face down on the table, her hair in disarray.

Victor was flapping his hand about, not the one that I had pulled but the one Elizabeth had held. He seemed to be in some pain. Lavinia was still working to extract her own hand from Elizabeth's grip. Howard shook his head to clear it and looked dazed.

"Is anybody hurt?" asked Yang imperturbably.

"Can someone look at Elizabeth, please?" Lavinia asked.

Yang went to look at Elizabeth. There was a triangle chalked on the back of his chair that I had not seen before.

Elizabeth was unconscious. One of the ladies wafted smelling salts under her nose, and she twitched and came to, blinking and rubbing her face as though it had been stretched out of shape. The maid was on hand with a glass of water.

"I'm fine," Elizabeth said bravely. "I think." She looked pale and drained—literally drained, as though substance had been sucked out of her and she had lost pounds of weight.

"Did you catch any of the words?" Howard asked Victor.

"A few, I think. We'd better write them down as soon as

possible. Or you had—don't think I can write just now." Victor was still rubbing his wrist.

"He's more powerful than we thought," said Howard.

"A doctor for this woman would be advisable," said Yang, taking the glass from Elizabeth before she dropped it.

"Oh, dear." Something had gone out of Elizabeth's face, as if it were a lightbulb burned out by too much current. "I don't feel well. What happened?"

Victor said something to Howard in an undertone, inclining his head towards Yang. Evidently, they wondered if he might be connected with the séance running out of control.

"Excuse me, but I'm afraid I may need a doctor, too," said Lavinia, holding the hand that had been crushed in Elizabeth's grip. "I'm afraid I may have broken some fingers."

Chapter Five

Of the Sorcerer Roslyn D'Onston

"You have read the leaflets on Theosophy," Yang said.

As usual, he was driving, and I was navigating. He was wearing a new salt-and-pepper suit in the American style with a dark-red bow tie, and a Fedora. And alligator shoes, and dark glasses, an affectation I had only seen in pictures of Hollywood actors.

Yang never said as much, but I had finally twigged that he did not, could not, read a single word of English. In spite of his obvious education and literacy in his own language, he had a sort of word-blindness when it came to the English alphabet. That made it even more curious that he had come alone without any assistant. It was not my place to ask questions. I simply made sure I was available to do any reading that was necessary without causing embarrassment.

"I read some of them," I said. "It's strange to me, all that business about Lemuria and Atlantis and Hyperborea and those other old kingdoms. It's worse than the Bible with the Moabites and the Elamites and the rest of them. If you know that lot."

"Please go on."

"Atlantis sank under the waves in a battle between good and bad magicians, so they say," I said. "According to Theosophy, every so often the bad magicians get the upper hand, and the whole lot goes under one way or another. The thing is, though—this 'magic' is a cosmic force called Vril, a bit like electricity..."

"Indeed?"

"But Vril was just a made-up thing. I don't know if the

novels of Mr Edward Bulwer-Lytton have been translated into Chinese? Bulwer-Lytton invented Vril in a book called *The Coming Race*, as a matter of fact."

I would never have believed that reading adventure novels would give me the chance to sound learned, but this was a topic on which I could be authoritative. I wanted to add that Bulwer-Lytton was the originator of the phrase about the pen being mightier than the sword—a doubtful proposition, to my mind—but felt that this would be lost on someone from China.

"It seems to me—only from reading those pamphlets—that Theosophy mixes up fact and fiction all higgledy-piggledy. Vril isn't real, and I'm sure Atlantis was never a real place. They have these dreams and visions, and they write them down as if they're true. On top of that—and they don't say it in as many words—Mrs Blavatsky cheated with at least some of her psychic effects."

Yang took his time before replying. At length, he took out his cigarette case; instead of taking a cigarette, he passed it over to me.

"Look."

The case was worked with an intricate pattern, a circle made up of curved shapes like two fish wrapped around each other: a dark fish with a light eye, and a light fish with a dark eye.

"This distinction is false. Night and day give rise to each other. Good and evil are not opposites but complementary. Shadow cannot exist without light. What you call fact and fiction are intertwined and cannot be separated. They support each other. They are 'two sides of the same coin,' as you say in English."

This might have been ancient Oriental philosophy, but it seemed like muddled thinking to me, and dangerous at that.

"Good and evil are two different things."

"Indeed? As a boxer, you fight people who you do not hate. In your work, you take money from people who you pity to give to rich people you despise. You deal with criminals like Mr Renville and do not report them to the police."

Yang smiled faintly as my discomfiture. I did not know where he had heard the name of Arthur Renville, but it was not from me. Nor had I mentioned that I collected debts.

"What did you make of that séance then?" I asked quickly, handing the case back to him.

I had gone over the events in my mind a hundred times and was less sure than ever about what I had seen. Lavinia's enthusiasm for getting patronage from a wealthy American was plain. Yang was also moneyed. Perhaps they had planned to stage an event to impress him. Theatrical smoke and sound effects, along with the power of suggestion, might have explained everything I witnessed. It is not unknown for mediums to be overcome with hysteria, perhaps even an infectious hysteria. That was more or less the version of events that I had agreed on with Arthur and Reg at our evening debriefing.

Perhaps it was my previous experience that made me think that magic is not so unlikely as all that, or maybe it was working in a Law firm. A man can stand up in court and say 'Habeas Corpus' and it changes everything. The right 'Hocus Pocus' might work just as well, with the laws of the natural world rather than human laws. Arthur and Reg maintained these laws they were two different things, but I was not so sure.

"A most curious event," said Yang. "The manifestation was unusual."

"Was it… real?"

Yang laughed sharply. "Real and unreal, dark and light—everything is dualism for you! Do you forget the pattern so quickly?"

"The manifestation—was it dangerous?"

"Perhaps."

"Did I do the right thing, pulling your hands apart from Howard's?"

"Who can say? Right and wrong is more dualism… now, please, which turning here?"

We had an appointment in Upper Norwood Library. It was one of the more compact sort of Victorian libraries and one that I had made use of on occasion. The library was doing its usual quiet trade. A scattering of people browsed the shelves while the reading tables were fully occupied—some pensioners but also several younger men hunched over the Jobs Vacant sections of the library newspapers.

Although I did not know whom we were meeting, Yang had again decided that I should come along—as though he wished me to be seen with him.

Yang consulted a note and led the way to the last alcove on the left, where a bearded man was absorbed in his studies at a round table, open books piled up around him. He was an odd individual, his beard long and ragged and his shoulder-length hair tied back in bohemian style. He had no jacket, just a colourless linen shirt a size too large for him with a rag of a tie and reading glasses mended with copper wire. He looked the sort of man who was too busy with higher things to take any trouble over his appearance and undid the work of any wife or valet who tried to set him straight.

He was looking from one to book to another, lost in his work. I coughed politely. And he looked up.

"Gentlemen, gentlemen!" he said at once, standing up and offering his hand. "Delighted to see you. My name is Powell."

Yang stood with his hands behind his back and nodded slightly. I made up for the deficiency and shook hands, introducing both of us.

"Make yourselves comfortable," said Powell, pulling out two chairs. "My library is your library. It's a pleasure to meet other students of Roslyn D'Onston. "

"As students, we are novices," said Yang, suddenly humble. He took out a notebook and a silver fountain pen. "We are honoured that you interrupt your work for a few minutes to share your knowledge with us. Please permit me to record your words."

"The honour is all mine," Powell beamed, and I saw he was missing a tooth.

"All aspects of Roslyn D'Onston are fascinating," said Yang. "But my purpose today is in what occult powers he claimed to possess and who his teacher was."

"So I gather—a most unusual interest!" Powell unfolded a grubby sheet of paper. "To start at the beginning… as a young man, he travelled to Paris in the 1860s to study medicine. He became acquainted with young Edward Lytton, son of Sir

Edward Bulwer-Lytton. When he showed an interest in the occult arts, he was introduced to the older gentleman, who initiated him into the Hermetic Mysteries."

"Bulwer-Lytton the famous novelist?" I said, astonished to hear the name again.

"The same," added Powell. "Properly, Lord Lytton, of course. Known to the public for his works of fiction but also a magist of considerable reputation. The account of magic in some of his works is correct—have you read *Zanoni*?"

"Please, Mr Powell," said Yang. "Tell us more of D'Onston. But you call him Stephenson?"

"His real name was Robert D'Onston Stephenson, but he went more often by Roslyn D'Onston," said Powell. "I use that name to avoid confusion with Robert Louis Stephenson."

"Another popular author—*The Case of Jekyll and Hyde*," I supplied.

"D'Onston studied medicine in Paris and chemistry in Hamburg, while there he carried out experiments of a psychical nature and dabbled in hypnotism. He served as a doctor with Garibaldi in 1860 and sought out witches in Italy; in West Africa he had a sort of apprenticeship with a witch doctor. After that, would you believe, he had a post with the Customs in Hull. That went sour when he was shot… so he went to India to study the occult."

Yang was busy taking notes. I was fascinated by the neatly composed Chinese characters flowing from his pen and forming columns of miniature hieroglyphs.

"He returned to London and took up with the Theosophists. He formed a romantic attachment with Mabel Collins, secretary of the Theosophists, Madame Blavatsky's assistant. That was when he was in Norwood, of course." Powell gave me a significant look.

"At this time, he wrote a number of articles for *Lucifer*, the Theosophy journal, under the pen name Tautridelta." Powell displayed a cheap-looking magazine. "These were chiefly about Black Magic, a subject on which he was recognised as a leading expert."

"Do you know what powers he claimed to possess?" Yang asked.

"I started to compile a list for you," said Powell. "Some of them are just street tricks. There's levitation—rising into the air—and being thrust through with a metal sword without being harmed, which he got from a fakir. But then there's this—he forced a witch in Sicily to give him the secret of a green ointment which, applied to the nerves above the eyes, gave the power of the fatal glance. He said he could kill cats and dogs with one look!"

"Really?" I said.

"That's what he said," said Powell with a laugh. "I might take that with a pinch of salt. He wasn't a modest chap, and he liked stories. D'Onston said that in Germany, he was able to swap minds with a fellow student. While he was in the other man's body, he went out and made love to his fiancé."

"Indeed," said Yang.

Powell stopped suddenly. I turned to follow his look. Behind me, a woman in a plain brown dress was going down the shelves, looking for a particular author. She took out a book, examined it, replaced it again, and selected another. Powell waited for her to go before continuing.

"In Africa, he was apprenticed to a sorceress called Sube," said Powell. "He claimed she was the original for Rider Haggard's *She*."

"That's another popular novel," I added for Yang's benefit.

"Sube could kill a man at four hundred paces, make plants grow in minutes and transform men into half-bestial creatures for pagan orgies." He was leafing through a book, finding a marked passage. "And more surprising yet, listen to this:

"'But the most terrible example of her power, to my mind, was in the transformation of the sexes. One day, being offended with a chief, who sought in vain to pacify her, she said to him, 'I will degrade you, and you shall become a woman!' Placing her hands upon him while he stood powerless as though turned to stone—his eyeballs staring in horror—she commenced her manipulations.'"

Powell paused for effect. He enjoyed having an audience.

"'Beginning with his face, she rubbed away every vestige of beard and moustache. The prominent cheekbones fell in, and the smooth, rounded face of a woman became apparent. Next, the powerful biceps and triceps were rubbed down, and the lank lean arm of the African woman appeared. Next, seizing hold of his vast pectoral muscles, she began a different process, pinching up and pulling them out until there were shortly visible, well-developed mammae. And so she proceeded, from head to foot, until, in less than ten minutes, every vestige of manhood had disappeared, and there stood before us a hulking, clumsy, knock-kneed woman.'"

"Indeed," said Yang. He had stopped taking notes.

While Powell was talking, I happened to look down at his shoes. The soles were secured to the uppers with lengths of twine, and they were battered and scuffed far beyond the ordinary degree. Powell was not simply an impoverished scholar who paid little attention to his appearance; he was an actual tramp. When I sniffed, I could detect the smell of the gutter common to all men of that type.

Powell was explaining to Yang how D'Onston could project scenes of history in the air by means of the fourth dimension and how this was a fact of science as well as scripture. For all his rough appearance, he spoke like a scholar. You could tell he had not always been the man we saw here. I believe Powell had been a respectable man once, a dry-goods wholesaler or some such. He had read an article about Jack the Ripper and then a book; it had become a hobby and then an obsession. The rest of his life had dropped away. Just from looking at him, you knew he did not have a home, a family, or a steady occupation anymore. All he had was this obsession, and it was meat and drink and family to him. This library had become his whole world. No wonder he was happy to admit others who shared the same interest.

I had an awful premonition of my own future. How far astray would I go from the broad, high road of normal life?

"But the blackest magic of all was that of Jack the Ripper." Powell proudly placed in front of me a piece clipped from the *Pall Mall Gazette*: "The Whitechapel Demon's Nationality: and Why He Committed the Murder" by "One Who Thinks He Knows."

Neither Yang nor I spoke, and Powell took this as licence to proceed, warming to his theme and speaking faster.

"D'Onston wrote this article and several others like it. He was the first to note that the murders were committed precise distances apart in a particular alignment. The murders were not committed by a homicidal maniac but by a perfectly sane and rational man: a magician following a recipe laid down by Eliphas Levi for raising the powers of Hell which required certain parts from a number of whores."

"Mass murder is not the act of a sane and rational man," I protested.

"It is when that man believes that he is on a higher plane, above good and evil," Powell countered. "Like artists and scientists, magicians don't care about the petty concerns that bother the rest of us. Humans are insects to them."

"You believe that D'Onston knew about Jack the Ripper?" said Yang.

Powell leaned forward, his voice dropping to a low, rapid murmur. "Yes, yes—look at the evidence! The timing, just after he had access to the Theosophist's library. D'Onston was at a hospital in Whitechapel when each of the murders was committed. He showed his friends how it was done without getting bloodied! He tried to persuade others that a Dr Davies—who didn't even exist!—was responsible. He wrote to the papers and persuaded another man to try and claim a reward from the police, giving him misleading clues... he was everywhere inside the investigation! They arrested him, but they couldn't make it stick—"

"Indeed, but what happened afterwards?" Yang asked, interrupting Powell's flow.

Powell shrugged. "There was an odd interlude when he set up a business with Mabel Collins in Baker Street selling a rejuvenating cream. Made from a secret formula! But... he was disillusioned with the occult after that. He started following Victoria Woodhull, the evangelist, and spent his last years on an original translation of the New Testament from original Greek and Latin Christian manuscripts. He held on to the occult way of thinking though. His notes on Holy Communion... consuming flesh and blood and gaining eternal life… I suppose we all dote on mortality close to the end."

"He's dead then," I said.

"Oh, yes. I can tell you for sure that Robert D'Onston Stephenson is dead. I have a copy somewhere here of the death certificate. 'Congestive heart failure' in 1912. A pity. I would like to ask him a few questions!"

Yang leaned forward in his chair. "You are certain he is dead?"

"Quite certain. I visited the grave."

"Indeed." Yang seemed to relax. "Roslyn D'Onston is dead."

The pause lengthened, and Powell looked from Yang to me.

"In that case," said Yang, "just one question remains. Could you kindly give us the address of the grave? It would be most interesting to visit it."

Powell looked puzzled then utterly horrified.

"We merely wish…" I started, thinking Yang had somehow offended him with the question.

Powell had turned completely ashen. His eyes rolled, and he made a dreadful sound like nothing I had ever heard. It was a long exhalation ending with a broken gurgle. It was, I now know, what is called a death rattle as the last air leaves a man's lungs. When he fell backwards into his chair, Powell the tramp-scholar was quite dead. I knew it before Yang put two fingers to the man's throat to feel for a pulse.

The thought must have occurred to Yang and me at the same time. Powell had been looking at something behind us when he died. We stood as one and hurried back through the library. There was no fleeing figure for us to pursue down Westow Street. If there had been anyone whose glance had been death to Powell, they could have stepped quietly into one of the many alcoves in the library and pretended to browse the shelves. Yang and I looked down the aisles as we passed, but there were no familiar faces.

By unspoken agreement, we left the library and continued without a word until we were back in the car. Yang took out his cigarette case, placed a cigarette between his lips, and as an afterthought, offered me one. I declined.

"I may now explain some of my purpose here. In Shanghai, there used to be an occultist, once an associate of Roslyn D'Onston, who fled from Europe. He made himself an enemy of the Si Fan. It was necessary for him to be killed."

Yang drew smoke and released it contemplatively.

"The occultist was suffocated to prevent his soul from escaping his body. His remains were placed inside a brass urn, which was sealed and kept under guard. One year later, nothing remained in the brass urn but maggots. The maggots were separated into seven portions and taken away to be fed to the fish of Seven Rivers."

I imagined the fish slipping away, disappearing like smoke into the endless water of the rivers.

"In this way, we were assured that no trace was left of the body. No tomb, burial site—not even ashes. We did this because it is believed that a sorcerer may return if such precautions are not taken."

"A very thorough job," I said. I could have asked what they did with the bones. Bone meal fed to the fish, I shouldn't wonder.

"The dead man received a letter in cipher in Shanghai a few weeks ago. It was signed with the name of Roslyn D'Onston. The return address was Maycot in Norwood. We had believed D'Onston to be dead; it is necessary to discover whether this is the case."

"Could I enquire about the contents of the letter?"

Yang gave me a sidelong look. I wondered if I was being impertinent, and perhaps it was not my place to ask, but he answered just the same.

"He asked questions about a certain occult process, seeking confirmation for the correct element for a successful outcome—a question of blood. In addition... to curry favour with the sorcerer, D'Onston confessed to a crime against the Si Fan which was previously only suspected."

"The letter cannot really have been from D'Onston. It must have been one of the others. Powell was convinced D'Onston was dead, and he had taken pains to check the fact."

As I said it, though, I was uncomfortably aware that Powell's own death looked much like the result of the evil eye that he attributed to D'Onston.

Yang contemplated the cloud of smoke slowly turning on itself and dispersing. "Indeed."

Chapter Six

A Banquet and a Battle

The next morning, Yang produced a slip with an address in the East End.

"A Chinese establishment," I said.

"There are formalities to be observed," said Yang. I was sufficiently attuned now to recognise his tone as one of resignation. He conveyed his meaning not so much by what he said as by what he did not say, if that makes any sense. "A visit is required to pay my respects to a family of importance."

He smoothed his goatee thoughtfully. "It would be beneficial if you were to accompany me. It will increase your experience of the life of the Chinese people. You may also have the opportunity to eat Chinese food."

"I don't know if I'm up to a social engagement." I was conscious of my appearance. I did not feel ready to meet any family of importance, English or Chinese. They would stare at my shabby suit and missing ear.

Yang barked a laugh. "All foreigners are ugly giants with big noses and strange clothes to the Chinese. Do not be concerned. You will not be in any way different to other English to them."

Yang flicked an invisible speck off his lapel, straightened his cuffs, and rang the doorbell.

A middle-aged Chinese woman in a plain blue smock ushered us in. She showed us through to a dim chamber decorated in the Oriental style with wooden screens worked with cranes and lotuses, bamboo matting, and low tables of dark wood.

Three men, also Chinese, were waiting for us, sitting cross-legged on the floor. They were dressed in what I imagined to be traditional fashion—wearing silk smocks, their hair in long pigtails—and looked as grave as a row of carved Buddhas.

Yang removed his hat and sat down in the same style; I did likewise with some small difficulty. A servant placed steaming cups of tea in front of each of us.

"The tea is merely symbolic," Yang murmured. "Do not drink it."

The three men started firing questions at Yang. Their tone seemed hostile at first, but perhaps the harsh, staccato nature of the language made it sound more so. Yang replied at some length in exactly the same tone. None of them touched their teacups, which presently stopped steaming.

This went on for some time, and I was studying the pattern on the nearest screen, admiring the workmanship—it was a good cedarwood piece and crafted to the last degree of detail—when one of the men suddenly addressed me in English. "It is true you are assisting Yang here?"

"As far as possible, yes."

"You saw a man die yesterday?"

"I'm afraid I did."

"Will you describe the occasion?" he asked.

I endeavoured to tell them how the unfortunate Powell had died, providing as much circumstantial detail as possible—even though they must only have been seeking to corroborate what Yang had already told them.

"Thank you," said the second man when I had finished. "A friend of Yang is a friend of ours. We are grateful for your assistance."

The three of them looked so much alike that I assumed they were brothers. The conversation switched back to Chinese. I resumed my study of the screen until suddenly the others were standing up.

"We have completed our explanations, and they have been accepted," said Yang. "There will follow some refreshment."

I followed them into a larger, better-lit room with silk cushions. There was a whole Chinese family of a dozen or more gathered there, from little children to a wizened old grandmother, and tables spread with covered dishes of all shapes and sizes. They waited for the men to sit down before taking their places. I was the subject of much scrutiny. They may not have seen many people of my size and bulk; I towered over the largest of the men. I did not meet their eyes but looked around, taking in colourful details of decoration and clothing. The women wore the tiniest slippers—I had never seen such small feet.

It was early for lunch, but everyone set to with a good appetite. This presented a challenge to me. The only cutlery was a pair of chopsticks, slender wooden rods that they deftly held together in one hand, picking morsels of food as easily as if they were using a fork or a pair of tongs. But after some experimentation, I could still not see the trick of it. So I could only watch as the others chattered around me, picking up this item and that without any effort. They must have noticed my difficulty but were too polite to offer assistance.

Yang ate sparingly, and though the three brothers were relaxed and at their ease, joking casually among themselves, he sat with stiff formality, nibbling at his food without enthusiasm. I was resigned to not eating when a small girl, perhaps six years old, noticed my difficulty. With the utmost seriousness, she left off tending to her infant brother and came over to show me the correct use of chopsticks.

"Like this, see?" she kept saying.

Unfortunately, I could still not get the knack of it after repeated demonstrations. Everything I tried to pick up fell back into the dish or onto the table. Undeterred, she held my fingers in place with both her hands and helped me steer a piece of meat into my mouth.

The little girl was as pleased as if she had been feeding buns to an elephant at the zoo. One of the grandmothers cackled with laughter at the sight while the child's mother and aunts clapped. Two small boys joined in excitedly, not used to such entertainment at mealtime. We repeated the maneuver, and to the entertainment of all, I sampled every dish on the table this way.

"Try this one!"

During this process I introduced myself. She told me that her name was Chun Hua. "That's my Chinese name," she added offhandedly. "In English I'm Spring Flower. I can write it in English and Chinese."

Various increasingly awkward foodstuffs were pushed forward as challenges to our combined skill. The rice was glutinous and easier than you would expect; slivers of some pale vegetable needed to be gripped firmly; crunchy nuggets had to be handled more gently, or they popped up into the air, occasioning laughter in the audience. Each success was met with applause for the little girl and her performing beast.

I cannot describe the flavours, which were pungent and savoury. I recognised pork and chicken in the meats and some offal as well. Most of it was entirely strange to me. Perhaps others would have been put off by the bowl of deep-fried chickens' feet, but as a butcher's boy, I was less delicate than most. Even the rice was mixed with bits of seafood. The mushrooms I knew but not the other vegetables—some crisp as cucumber, others melting like well-cooked asparagus, and all seasoned in unexpected ways.

Yang's fixed expression signified disapproval. And yet, as the performance continued, he seemed to soften. He even smiled as a crisply fried prawn, spicy with hot pepper, reached my mouth on the third attempt, to a fresh round of applause.

I never mastered the use of chopsticks without assistance, but my little helper didn't tire of the experience of aiding a grown-up. She wanted to help me lift a teacup to my lips and was disappointed that I was capable of drinking without assistance. When I managed to assure her that I had eaten enough, she bowed politely and returned to her mother's side.

I parted with the Chinese family on the most cordial of terms in spite of the lack of common language, and there was much bowing and smiling, which I imitated.

"I hope my behaviour was acceptable," I said soon as we were out of earshot.

"They are exceptionally well-bred. You could never offend them," he said coldly.

Yang would have left it at that, but I wanted to find out more. "It was a most interesting experience, as you promised. I enjoyed having a traditional Chinese meal. They seem a nice family."

"They are a traditional family of old China," he said with such unmistakable contempt that I looked up. "In Shanghai, we do not wear our hair in a queue and wear old clothes. We do not sit on the floor—and English guests are offered a knife and fork."

"Some people like their colourful traditions."

"Colourful traditions like killing female children? In China, we find many daughters die of a scorpion sting while they are in the cradle. Chun Hua is lucky there are few scorpions in England! But they are not binding her feet; maybe even the old dragon learns at last."

I held my tongue.

"Now, I have a further formality to complete with others who may be less sympathetic. Please direct us to this address. This visit I will conduct on my own."

I was not so familiar with this part of London, and we stopped twice to ask directions but found our way easily enough. Yang left me sitting in the car while he disappeared into an ordinary-looking, big house. I was content enough to digest my lunch and reflect on the exotic dining experience.

After half an hour, I began to wonder how long Yang would be. He had given no indication, but some inner barometer warned me that something was awry. When he said that these people were less sympathetic, I suspected he might have been understating the case. I decided to stretch my legs and walk past the house a couple of times. It was a four-storey villa with steps leading up to the front door. On my second pass, I saw a grey object by the basement windows beside the stairs. It was Yang's hat.

Another man might have worked his way round the back and clambered over the garden wall. I wasn't a great one for clambering or shinnying up drainpipes or any other cat-burglar tricks. Instead, I took the frontal approach.

A Chinese man in an English shirt and waistcoat opened

the door. He did not look friendly.

"I beg your pardon," I said, "but I'm looking for Mr Yang."

"Never heard of him," he said in an East End accent. He jerked his head. "Now, get lost."

That was uncalled for. I did not care for his language and was about to tell him so when there was an unmistakable cry of pain from within the house. It sounded like Yang.

The rude man glanced back over his shoulder at the noise. He knew the game was up, and he started to draw a weapon from behind him. That was not a wise move. By the time he had pulled out what looked like a jointed wooden cosh, I had one hand around his forearm and the other gripping a fistful of his shirtfront. Without pausing to formulate a plan, I hauled him bodily out of the door and threw him towards the pavement. While he was still stumbling down the stairs, I stepped smartly through the door and had it bolted behind me before he reached the ground.

The cry appeared to have come from above. I moved swiftly through the hall and up the stairs two at a time, stepping as lightly as I could. From the landing I saw Mr Yang through an open doorway. He was in a chair, facing me. His hands were bound behind him; his face was bruised. His shirt had been torn open at the neck.

A man with his back to me turned partly and rapped out a question in Chinese. He was holding a sharpened piece of bamboo the size of a pencil in one hand. As he turned, I saw he was also Chinese and had a livid scar down one cheek.

I registered another person in the room, sitting in the far corner. A card table had been pushed against the wall to make more space, and a number of objects were arranged on it—more bamboo skewers, a crumpled cloth, Yang's cigarette case, and a compact automatic pistol.

This was no time for questions. I stepped in and gave the scarred man a straight right between the eyes. The blow knocked him on to the table, which tipped over.

The man in the corner was getting to his feet—not that quickly, because he was a very fat man, but not as slowly as all that. He was not just fat; he was big all round, practically a giant by Chinese standards, and there were powerful muscles underneath the rolls of flab. He had a scarf around his waist instead of a belt, and his shirtsleeves were rolled up, showing thick forearms covered in oriental tattoos.

His eyes were almost closed. For a moment, I thought that it was because his face was so fat, then I realised that he could not see. I relaxed for an instant, and the blind man, hearing my sigh, half-smiled. Then he lowered his head and charged right at me. I threw a quick left, which simply glanced off his shoulder, and then we were grappling.

Clinches are a part of the art of boxing, and you have to know how to use them to your advantage. But wrestling is another matter.

The fat man had a grip like a steel clamp, and I felt my ribcage grinding. That grip would have crushed the life out of most of his opponents but not one of my physique. My arms were free, and I was able to jab at his head and neck with sharp, quick punches. He let go with a grunt and stepped back.

Yang was still sitting in the chair, dazed. The scarred man was getting to his feet, grabbing a handful of pointed bamboos, until I clubbed him heavily over the back of the neck with the side of my fist.

The wrestler turned his head this way and that, still smiling faintly. He was the scarred man's hired muscle as surely as I was Yang's. We were put to fighting each other to see who the better man was. And if he was blind, it didn't seem to affect his ability to come straight at me again like a charging bull.

There was not enough space to dodge him properly or back off. In the ring, I would have been able to keep him off and rain punches on him all the while. It was a different story in a confined space.

I was carried backwards two paces into the wall. The impact shook plaster dust loose. His grip was lower this time, below my ribs. I got in two awkward blows, hammering downwards on his head. Then the wrestler straightened up and did a move that I had not experienced since I was ten years old: he threw me clean over his shoulder. I would not have said it was possible… I dived headlong, my feet struck a light fixture, and the room tumbled about me. My landing felt as though it made the house shake.

They say you could drop an ant from the top of St. Paul's and it would walk away unhurt, but an elephant would be injured by the slightest fall because of its great bulk. In this respect, I am more elephant than ant. The force of the impact was considerable. If I'd landed worse, I could have broken an arm or a wrist or my neck. I was lucky not to crack my head on a stone mantel or fireplace.

Luck was with me, though, and I landed flat. Acting on instinct, I rolled and pulled myself to a crouch. A sighted opponent might have thrown himself down on top of me before I could move, and that might have been the end of it. He would have been on top of me, his hands round my head, and there would be no escape. But the confusion of noises made it difficult for the blind wrestler to locate me exactly, and he hung back.

We faced each other again. I needed to end the fight quickly before the man I had thrown down the stairs could make his way back in and before anybody else in the house could join in—I could hear voices downstairs. The fat man's smile was fixed. He reminded me of someone I had seen once, a slaughterman my father had pointed out to me once. He was an odd character, and Father said that the man enjoyed killing a bit too much and I had best stay away from him. The wrestler had that selfsame cold, complacent smile of pleasure at suffering.

I took a half step forward to jab at his face, left and right. I would make him earn his money, at least, and buy enough time to try something else. A clinch was the only way he could keep from being beaten black and blue, and this time, I planned to throw myself out of his path as soon as he came forward.

His hand moved like a striking cobra and caught my left wrist. It was like being trapped in a vice. I directed a straight right at his shoulder, and the grip lessened. As well as an ungodly strength, he must have had iron self-control not to flinch at the pain. His other arm moved over to foul my next punch.

I have often wondered how the fight would have proceeded from that point on. When you review a bout in your mind, you always think of the moves that you might have done if you were given a second chance, if the fight had only run to another round.

My supporters might say that Harry Stubbs could beat any Chinese, but you have to look at the facts behind the bravado. I had a few more tricks in my repertoire, but I'm a boxer. All my routines were ingrained through long hours of training that turned them into reflex actions. And they are all boxing moves. If a man wants to stand toe-to-toe in any approximation of boxing, I know what to do. But the arts of grappling, of holds and throws and breakfalls, of knowing where to twist an arm or a wrist or a neck, are all comparative mysteries to me. I am a boxer of more than average mettle, but I am not a fighter.

The wrestler was a real fighter. He knew how to play the game in which the only rule was to win. It was a game that I had little experience of, and this was no way to learn.

The fight was interrupted by the sharp crack of a pistol shot. Yang was still sitting, but now he had his hands in front of him. He was aiming the automatic at the fat man. At the time, it did not occur to me that what made the wrestler stop was not the threat of the pistol but the sound of the report. For those who rely on hearing, a loud noise in a small room is like a dazzling light in the eyes of a sighted person.

"Mr Stubbs, we must leave," Yang said. I did not need to be told twice. He said something sharp in Chinese at the fat man while I hurried back down the stairs. There were two men at the bottom, but they scattered when Yang fired at their feet.

I unbolted the front door. There was no sign of the rude individual whom I had manhandled earlier, and we made it clear to the car. Nobody was pursuing us. This was a London street in broad daylight after all.

Yang sat heavily in the driver's seat and put down the pistol. He held his hands out to me. His thumbs were fastened together with wire; I untied it with some difficulty. Then Yang felt cautiously around one of the bloodstains on his shoulder, and I saw for the first time what looked like a pencil stub sticking from low down on neck. With a grimace, he pulled out a bamboo skewer and tossed it into the footwell. A moment later, he pulled out a second.

"My second appointment was less successful than the first," he said at last. "There has been some... misunderstanding between the Si Fan and the Yellow Emperor's Clan."

They had ambushed Yang on the steps before he could even knock on the door. The blind man had come up from behind, seized Yang, and thrown him to the ground before he knew what was happening. He never had a chance to draw his gun.

Yang raised and lowered his injured arm experimentally, frowning at the result. "I will require your assistance with the handbrake and the gears."

Chapter Seven

A Warning

That evening, with Yang safely back in his hotel room and having devoured a healthy portion of my landlady's steak and kidney pudding, I raided the cigar box under my mattress for money. Shillings jingling in my pocket, I made my way to the Conquering Hero. I had earned a pint or two, or three or four. The place was as warm and cheerful as you could wish, half-full with the usual weekday crowd.

I nodded to a few acquaintances while the barman drawing my pint said casually, "Feller over by the corner is looking for you, Harry. Funny sort of bloke."

As he spoke, my eye fell on Howard, the scholarly young man of the Theosophy Circle. He was sitting alone at a table with a shot glass and a decanter of water. He had witnessed my entrance and looked up expectantly.

"I know him," I said.

"Don't think he comes in pubs much," said the barman. "He wanted hot water with it. I haven't heard that since before the war."

"I'm so glad you came," said Howard, pulling up a chair for me. He pushed back his thinning hair with one hand. "The situation is grave, and you're the only man alive who can help."

"I'm afraid I don't know what situation you're referring to."

"Don't worry, old man," he said. "I'm not with the police or anything. But I don't think you came to the séance the other day out of idle curiosity, and I happen to know a little about your connections." He glanced about as though the Hero was a notorious thieves' den. "The thing is, I know what you're on to, and I can help."

"Is this in reference to Mr Roslyn D'Onston?" I ventured.

"Absolutely right; you've got it in one," he said with a fierce smile. "Roslyn D'Onston, that notorious creature, unparalleled master of the dark arts. You know of his infiltration of the Theosophy Circle?"

"I had ascertained some connection."

"Connection? He's in charge of it! You do realise of course that he isn't dead?"

"Well, I can't say..."

"Let me lay the whole thing out for you." He leaned closer. "As you know, I'm just a poor bookworm. I've dabbled in the arts for a few years, as an intellectual exercise—in a field where there are so few true scholars, an amateur like me can earn a little distinction. And then out of the blue, I have an approach from this woman, the one who calls herself Lavinia.

"It seems that she's turned up out of nowhere and is occupying that house, Maycot—Blavatsky's place and D'Onston's former base of operations. Well, that ought to have made me suspicious. And with her is this Victor. His bona fides are in India and not so easy to check."

"It should be possible to telegraph India—"

"Good Lord. Don't you realise how easy it is to pass for another man these days? I don't say Victor is a fiction, but I doubt very much whether our Victor is the genuine article. Though he is damnably well-informed about Indian magic... but I'm getting ahead of myself."

He was certainly getting ahead of me in his hurry to get the story out.

"You were at the séance. You saw how dangerous that was, how the two of them play with fire? That was a damn fool thing to do and all because they want power." He gave a hollow laugh. "Power is a dangerous thing—you can turn the tap on, but if you can't turn it off again, then woe betide you!" He banged his empty glass down for emphasis.

"To start at the beginning..." I said.

"Of course," he said, nodding down at my glass, which was

still more than half-full. "Have another?"

He brought back a brandy with another pint for me and settled himself down. Howard spoke with a sure authority about everything. He seemed very relaxed in a strange place like this, and even when talking to a stranger like me with such frankness. I expected a scholar to be a mousy, bookish sort of man, more hesitant when outside his own academic sphere. But for all that he looked like a librarian, Howard spoke like a brigadier.

"It was my fate—I won't say misfortune, or fortune—to come into my inheritance early. My parents left enough money for a comfortable existence without the need to earn bread with the sweat of my brow. And don't think that I'm not grateful for that every day of my life." He seemed concerned that I might resent his wealth. "That has given me the leisure and the resources to make a study of certain arts. I've made little enough progress, I can tell you. I've slaved over incomprehensible books, spent long nights at my workbench with queer mixtures of chemicals... and, in the morning, found I had nothing. But I've placed my poor offering on the great altar of Knowledge."

"You've written some important works, I gather."

"Hardly. A few monographs, published at my own expense. They brought me into contact with other scholars, and we corresponded. I know it sounds like a rather arid existence"—he seemed apologetic—"but it suited me well enough. Until, out of the blue, Lavinia contacted me. She insisted that I visit her and meet the Circle. Soon, I was caught up in a whole cycle of speaking engagements, social affairs, and séances. For the first time in my life, I was feted as a celebrity. It was heady stuff for a man who has lived his life in quiet seclusion, and I told them everything I knew—far more than I should have done. That was before I realised how dangerous Lavinia and Victor really were—before I heard the name Roslyn D'Onston."

He paused to gulp brandy and confirm that I understood what he was saying.

"These people," he said, "these people are not the selfless seekers after knowledge that they pretend to be. Roslyn D'Onston wants to harness the ultimate powers of darkness... I expect you know all about him?"

Now it was up to me to play my part, to make quick deductions and bluff my way through the interview. "I know very little of him. But my major conclusions have been, firstly, that he has been deceased for some years, and secondly, that he experienced a Christian awakening and turned his back on black magic. So, while the influence of his older self may live on, along with his assumed name, I don't see that we are dealing with the actual gentleman."

Howard bit his lip. "I assure you," he said levelly, "that Roslyn D'Onston is far from dead and far from reformed. And he is brewing up a foul scheme that will be, dare I say it, injurious to your interests. I know these things from my own, first-hand experience—and that is why I am now in fear for my life. You see, I heard about what happened in the library with poor old Powell yesterday."

A vagrant dying of natural causes in a public library was hardly the stuff of news headlines, and the story had not been in the papers. Howard saw my questioning look.

"One of the members of our Circle was in the library this morning, and they're talking of nothing else. Naturally, I asked Victor and Lavinia, and they were so cryptic about it that I came right out and asked if they thought there was skulduggery involved. Victor hinted darkly and even mentioned that little trick with green ointment—the death gaze that D'Onston described so vividly in his work on the evil eye in Sicily."

"And that is why you are in fear for your own life," I said.

He nodded vigorously. "I know too much about their plans, their *modus operandi.* And I even suspect… but tell me, before I go further… I shan't ask who you're working with or who you report to, but can I know that you'll get word back to headquarters and steps will be taken against that pair?"

He was putting me in a false position entirely. Like Victor, Howard had read some significance into my possessing the ring with the green star-stone, and that had been further magnified. He must have known of my presence in the library with Yang—we were such an unlikely pair that he would know us from the sketchiest description—and had obviously linked us together as agents of some occult grouping. Instead of being a debt collector and sometime clerk, I was part of a conspiracy. Given that I was working with Yang, who was a bona fide member of the Si Fan Society, he was not so far from the truth.

"I can't guarantee action," I said. "That decision would be taken by the appropriate persons."

Howard flashed an easy smile. "Of course, of course. Though I dare say you might have a hand in action that does get taken, what?"

I gave a modest half nod, and he launched into the next part of his address. "I did a few calculations. I dare say you did the same—Roslyn D'Onston would be eighty-three years old this year. Of course he didn't die." He waved the idea away as though it was an irritating fly. "As a doctor, D'Onston had endless access to medical forms, and there's nothing easier than slipping a death certificate into the records. He could have acquired a body easily enough if he actually needed to fill a coffin."

"And you think he's now operating under the name of Victor? But D'Onston's much too old to be him."

"Think on," he said, "and you'll see another possibility. Wouldn't you say that Lavinia is rather mannish, rather tall and masculine looking? She's the right age. To D'Onston, flesh is simply clay that he can mould to his will. Male and female are mutable to him, like Tiresias of old."

He allowed the words to sink in a minute. "Now you see the diabolical genius of it. Who would ever suspect a harmless old lady who dabbles in spiritualism of being a famous black magician?"

"It's quite a proposition," I said. "And what is her, or should I say his, purpose?"

"You don't recall the days of Jack the Ripper, I suppose." Howard, who looked no more than thirty, had barely been born at the time, and surely his family did not discuss grisly murders at the dinner table. "It was a reign of terror like no other. Women were plucked from the streets in his grim harvest. All London was in an uproar. The Ripper slipped through the fingers of the police time after time. If he gained the power he sought"—his voice dropped to a breathless whisper—"he'd be capable of anything."

"You believe D'Onston is the Ripper then?"

"The Ripper showed what a man could do if he just had the will to see the thing through." Howard's eyes were bright, and he breathed louder. "D'Onston's power would multiply with his harvest. All London would be grist to that mill, all flesh living and dead, what transmutations might he not do…" He seemed excited and appalled at the same time.

"I see."

Howard kept looking at me expectantly, but after a minute, when I said nothing more, he nodded, interpreting my silence as the stoicism of a military man faced with a new mission.

"You know what to do, don't you?" He slid a small key across the table. "There, that's the back door key to Maycot. If you strike suddenly, you're sure to win—physically, she's just a weak woman. But you mustn't let her speak. One word, one look could be fatal. Now, I've already stayed too long. I must fly!"

With no more ado, he drained his glass and marched off, plucking his coat from the rack and flinging it around his shoulders as he passed—an exit worthy of the West End. It left me quite overwhelmed. Howard was not at all the man I had taken him to be.

"Evening, Harry." It was Reg, holding a glass and a bottle of Bass. The remnant of froth on his moustache indicated this was not his first beer. He nodded at the empty chair. "Mind if I…?"

I was grateful to see him, as he was someone who I could discuss the matters of the day with. I hoped he might help me get my muddled thoughts in order and make some sense of it all.

"I hear you've been chasing around the East End," he said, pouring his ale carefully. I have observed this eccentricity—of wanting to pour your own from the bottle—among several who have served overseas for long periods. "And Yang came to some harm in the process."

Arthur's spies had been keeping tabs on us. I gave Reg a brief account of the day. He nodded at parts of it, frowned at others.

"That sounds like the Wu brothers," he said, when I described the three members of my inquisition. "They deal in tea and silks coming one way, cotton and gin the other—a very prosperous business, by all accounts, and a noble family, too. Their father was the Emperor's cousin. That's why he had to go into exile."

"Exile—why?"

"Hardly germane to our present inquiry. What happened then?"

When I got to the scarred man sticking skewers into Yang and the fight with the wrestler, he let out a low whistle.

"That's a turn up for the books." Reg slapped me on the shoulder. "And you beat him man-to-man! Well, I never did… I'd heard stories, but never knew anyone who'd actually seen them. Xiongshoo Mang, the blind assassins, the death-dream-walkers! Good grief, Harry. "

He insisted in buying me a drink and explained that the blind men were a sort of mythical Thuggee sect that Chinese used for dirty work. These night stranglers were consecrated to an idol from childhood. They built up the strength in their wrists, and their tolerance for pain, by hanging from a bar for hours every day. They always carried out their killings under cover of darkness. They moved noiselessly, navigated by touch, finding their victims by the sound of their heartbeat and the warmth radiating from them. They could strangle a man and slip away without waking his sleeping wife next to him.

"That's a vile way to use blind children." I often passed the Normal School, where they taught the blind to be piano tuners.

"They're not blind when they start," said Reg. "It's an evil cult. They say no man ever faced the Xiongshoo Mang and lived. That may be an exaggeration, but still, you are a very lucky man, Harry. Or a very valiant one, I should say."

"Why did they need someone like him to apprehend a little fellow like Yang?"

"Never try to figure the Chinese out, Harry," Reg advised. "East is East…They've got wheels within wheels, and you'll always end up behind them. Their lot—the Yellow Emperor's Clan—torture Yang because his lot in the Si Fan have tortured one of their lot. Because their lot tortured one of his lot. It all comes out in the wash. These feuds go back centuries, and there's nothing you or I can do to stop them. That's something you have to learn. They've tumbled Yang now, and I don't expect he'll be staying here much longer if he knows what's good for him."

"You didn't tip them the wink, did you?"

"Not me!" Reg chuckled at the idea. "I tell you, the Si Fan never forget a grudge; they just keep adding to the list. The fellow that tipped them off—he'll be found one day, next week or next year or in ten years' time, with his tongue cut out by the Si Fan. They spy on each other and betray each other and torture each other. It will out sooner or later."

"Will they be after my blood?"

Reg sipped his ale thoughtfully before shaking his head. "They respect a strong man. You're just a hired soldier. Chinese soldiers change sides all the time depending who pays them, it's expected. But betrayal – that's another matter! Anyway, now he knows they're after him, I expect Yang will be off soon enough."

Reg seemed well satisfied when he left. For Reg, seeing the back of Yang would be enough to settle the matter, but I was not so sure. I did not think Yang was stirring up mischief. His object was Roslyn D'Onston. Powell struck stone dead in the library was a sign that D'Onston was alive, ruthless and in possession of uncanny powers. And if there was any truth in what Howard said, D'Onston would kill again and again in pursuit of some hidden purpose. It was difficult to put this in words for Reg, and Arthur would be equally dubious. Only Yang was likely to understand.

I was content enough when I made my way back home later that night, but my sleep was not a peaceful one.

I woke suddenly in the early hours, a thing I rarely do. Usually, you can tell what's woken you easily enough—a dustbin lid blown off, or fighting cats. I lay listening, but the night was completely still.

I rolled over to look at the luminous radium dials on the alarm clock. Something was wrong with the conformation of my bedroom, which seemed to press closer on me than it should.

The wall had moved somehow, or perhaps the wardrobe. I reached and switched on the bedside light.

Towering over me like a wall of flesh was the fat Chinese wrestler. He stood with his arms folded, big and motionless as a granite pillar. His face was bruised where I had hit him that afternoon.

At the click of the light switch, he unfolded his arms and reached for my throat. I jumped violently and woke up—really woke up this time. My room was empty. I checked under the bed and in the wardrobe and locked the door. Even then, I did not feel entirely safe. After I climbed back into bed, I kept opening my eyes at intervals to reassure myself that it had all really been a dream.

I got to thinking again about the fight with the wrestler and what I could have done and how I would defend myself if we were to meet again. There was the ice axe on my dressing table, but that was cumbersome for a close fight. Then I recalled some knuckle-dusters, which Arthur had issued me as a contingency for a particular job. I had never used them, knuckle-dusters being dangerous things to carry or use, and they had lain neglected ever since in a bottom drawer. I fetched them out and put them over my hands. They were cold at first but soon warmed, and the weight was a comfort.

I slept badly until the morning.

Chapter Eight

An Interview at the Convent

The next morning, Yang was in a charcoal-grey suit with narrow pinstripes, and apart from some stiffness in his shoulder, he looked as good as new. I know I never looked so well the day after a fight though, unlike Yang, I did not disguise the bruises on my face with powder. Iodine was as far as I ever went.

He was not his usual energetic self though. "Yesterday," said Yang quietly, "you rescued me from an unfortunate situation.."

I was painfully aware how embarrassing that must be for Yang. He had suffered the supreme loss of face of being humiliated in front of an inferior and then requiring that inferior's help. He was, in his own way, the proudest of men. The whole episode must have wounded his pride severely.

"Yes," I said. "I really am very sorry about that, Mr Yang."

Yang opened his mouth, and closed it again. Then he let out an unexpected bark of laughter. It must have been the look on my face as I apologised for saving his life that did it.

I laughed as well, but two seconds later Yang had resumed his poker face. There might just have been the faintest lines at the corners of his mouth. "I accept your apology, Mr Stubbs," he said at last and extended his hand.

We shook hands. Yang no longer had that long nail on his little finger. It must have broken off somewhere in the struggle.

"You fought well," he said simply.

I told him about my meeting with Howard the previous evening and how Lavinia had been unmasked as Roslyn

D'Onston—according to Howard anyhow. Arthur might not have appreciated my sharing that intelligence. On the other hand, Arthur had asked me to help Yang, and that was what I was doing.

"This places me in a difficult position," I said. "I need to know what action you plan to take with this person. But you understand that, whatever kind of feud your people may have with Roslyn D'Onston, the law here is still the law."

"In China, foreigners are not subject to Chinese law. If, for example, you were to murder someone in Shanghai, the local police could only hand you over to the British Embassy. A curious quirk of our colonial history." Yang spoke lightly but with animation. "Of course, the moral justice of the universe is another matter. Like water, it runs in its own way regardless of human concerns."

"That's as may be."

"Roslyn D'Onston shot a Chinese man in California over some gold," Yang added.

"That's a matter for the American authorities." It was a pompous thing to say.

Yang shook his head. "Mr Stubbs, Roslyn D'Onston is a very powerful individual—more powerful than Powell guessed. My many efforts have not located him; he leaves ripples, but that is all. He is as elusive as water in water." Like Jack the Ripper, I thought, who stayed invisible with all London looking for him. "If I were to confront this woman, I could prove nothing. And if she truly is D'Onston…" Yang shrugged. "The likely outcome would be my death."

"Why did you come here, if not for revenge?"

"My superiors wished to make D'Onston show himself. I could have arrived quietly. I did not need to advertise myself by sending a letter, and parading in distinctive clothes and car."

He took another drag on his cigarette, waiting to see if comprehension would dawn.

"They sent you as bait," I said. "That's a rotten thing to do."

Yang gave another shrug, indicating his life or death was not worthy of consideration. "There is a story about a traveller chased by a tiger to the edge of an abyss. The man took hold of a vine and started to climb down when he saw an angry dragon at the bottom of the abyss, and when he looked up, the tiger was lashing its tail above. As he hung on, a mouse started to gnaw away at the vine he was clinging to. The man was ready for death when he noticed a wild strawberry growing next to him, so he plucked it. It was the sweetest he had ever tasted."

Yang took a final puff and delicately crushed the stub of the cigarette into a china ashtray. Then he became business-like.

"Collins is gone, you said? This is unfortunate. It will be necessary to talk to the woman Sally. You described how she was assaulted before Collins drove off the assailant with a volley of shots. This may be an event of some importance."

"Why is that?"

"You will arrange an interview, and all will become clear."

"What about Lavinia?"

"It will not be profitable to meet with her at this point."

I recalled that Arthur had arranged for a cleaning job for Sally at the Virgo Fidelis convent. I went in search of him so he could help us set up a meeting. It was past ten o'clock in the morning, but Arthur had not yet retired to bed after his night's work. He was in the Electric Café with the telephone on the table in front of him. He had been much involved with handling a shipment of pineapples and had been able to shift almost all of them. With fresh fruit, there was no time to lose, and Arthur was fretting over the final few.

"Ham and pineapple," he said the moment he saw me, snapping his fingers. Evidently, the sight of me gave him an idea. "That's the way the Yanks eat it. Your esteemed father ought to be able to shift a few crates of pineapples if he sells them cheap with every order of ham."

"I don't know," I said doubtfully. I enjoy pineapple upside-down cake as much as the next man, but fruit and meat is a strange combination. It reminded me of the Chinese meal I had enjoyed the previous day—not the sort of thing normal English people were likely to sit down to.

"Well, maybe he can start a new fashion over here. I'll send him two crates on spec, and he can do what he likes with them." Arthur scribbled a note to himself. "Now, what can I do for you?"

I explained about Sally; Arthur did not seem surprised that Yang wanted to talk to her. "I'll make a phone call," he said. "What's the time now? Go round there at one o'clock, and you can talk to her then."

I had never been in Virgo Fidelis before. Most of it was given over to a girls' school, and we were directed to a room that must have been the head teacher's study or something like it. The walls were bare except for a wooden crucifix on one side facing a rather overly coloured picture of the Virgin Mary on the other.

Sally was waiting for us, her hands folded in her lap. She wore a long black skirt, a plain blouse, and no makeup. I hardly recognised her. She smiled timidly at me but wouldn't make eye contact with Yang.

"I'm a different woman now," she assured me. "I've left all that behind me."

She pushed her hair back with one hand. It was cut short now and kept falling in front of her face. Oddly, Sally looked younger than when I had seen her before.

"So I understand," I said.

"I don't know what you want to talk to me for," she said. "I can't remember nothing. I was drinking, and… I put it out of my mind."

"I told Mr Yang everything," I said. "I was there at the pub, you know."

"Were you? See, I didn't even remember that."

"I was there, and I heard what you said at the time. Except, at the time, you were in some distress and couldn't articulate too well. I thought, perhaps, with the passage of time, you might be able to tell us more easily."

Sally shook her head. "Sorry, it's like I said…"

Yang had taken a square of gold foil from his pocket. He dexterously unfolded it into a sort of Chinese lantern with tassels. It was on the end of a piece of twine, and spun to and fro as he rolled the string between his fingers.

"This may help," he said, holding it up and looking into the whirling golden bauble as if it were a crystal ball. "Look into the gold. See how it spins, how it catches the light. Look into it. Look to the light inside it."

Sally obediently looked at the bauble.

"We don't want anything from you, Sally," said Yang. "Just look into the light. Let your mind go. You must have been working very hard at your cleaning. Now you can relax for a bit. Just sit here and look at the golden lights going around and around."

I tore my gaze from the spinning bauble with difficulty. Sally was gazing deep into it, her eyelids heavy. For a moment, I wondered whether seconds had passed or hours.

"You like going to the cinema, Sally? Imagine you are there now, sitting in the back row. It is a comfortable seat. You are feeling relaxed. The movie that you are watching is a newsreel of that night. You see yourself on the screen, standing at the end of the alley. You are safe and comfortable, watching the screen. Your friend Collins is on the screen, too, waiting just around the corner. What do you see next?"

"There's a funny sort of man coming down the street," said Sally, picking up without hesitation. "You can see him as he goes from the streetlight to shadow, streetlight to shadow. He sort of shambles along." She rolled her shoulders in unconscious imitation of the peculiar gait. "He's tall and all covered up in a long coat. But not really, because it doesn't reach all the way down, him being so tall."

"Now the man in the long coat is approaching the Sally on the screen," said Yang. "We're watching it in the cinema, and it's a close-up of the two of them. What can we see?"

"I'm wearing my blue dress, and he comes right over, kind of slouching over and leaning on the wall right next to me."

"Can we see his face?" asked Yang, still twirling the golden bauble as Sally looked into it.

"Not at first. He's got a hat on, and it's all in shadows, and there's a scarf over his mouth, and I don't like that, either. I step back into the alley, not thinking, just because he's too close. Up close, he's so big I have to lean back to look at him."

"You're still watching on the screen, remember," said Yang.

"And he unwinds the scarf from around his face, and that's when I see it's Billy McCann. I'm so confused, because he's been dead two years. He steps into the alley—and I scream—"

"The cinema projector catches for a moment there," said Yang as Sally's voice was starting to rise. "So the image is frozen on the screen, and we can see what you saw. But it's on the screen, so he can't harm us."

Sally's expression softened again. She screwed up her eyes as though trying to make out a picture.

"It's dark in the alley because it's all in shadow, but that's why it's so scary. His arms are wrong—one of them is bigger than the other. But his face… he's got a hat on, and this scarf over his mouth, but I can see this bit." She ran a hand over her face at eye level, indicating that strip covered by a masquerader's mask. "That's why it's scary. It's dark, but I can see it because it's glowing except the eyes are like black holes. Glowing green like a corpse."

Sally stopped a moment, seeing that face again.

"And I scream, and he stops a moment like he's surprised, and Edward comes round the corner and shoots him, bang bang bang bang." She mimed a pistol with her hand. "I run out of the way and into the street and into the pub…"

"And then the lights come up," said Yang, "and that's the end of the film, and you're safe in the cinema. Comfortable and relaxed."

He kept twirling the golden bauble for another minute as Sally's breathing slowed back down to normal. Then he allowed it to come to a gradual stop.

"That was very interesting, Sally," he said, carefully folding up the gold foil. "You have my appreciation." He bowed slightly.

"And mine too," I added.

Sally looked from me to Yang and back.

"Is that it?" she asked.

"You have been very helpful," said Yang, standing up.

"Do you know what—who…?" She trailed off, looking confused. Yang merely smiled and bowed on his way out.

"It's a very peculiar case," I said.

To my surprise, Sally reached out and put a hand on my arm.

"Do be careful, Mr Stubbs."

Afterwards, Yang wanted to go back to the hotel. Evidently,

he was tired out by the whole experience and his shoulder pained him. He indicated that my services would not be needed for the rest of the day.

"Be ready tomorrow," said Yang. "Tomorrow, I think, we will discover some of the secrets of life and death."

Chapter Nine

The Death of Mr Yang

The hotel lounge was a comfortable place to hang around. I read the morning paper and back issues of *Punch* as well as talking to the clerk, Walker. He filled me in on Arthur's counter-intelligence operation keeping tabs on Yang.

"He burns things in his room," said Walker. "The bellboy got excited, thinking it was opium, but it's only joss sticks. Lord knows how we'll get the smell out."

"Is it worse than tobacco?"

"People don't mind cigarettes. And there's that cat. I don't know what we're going to charge him when he leaves, but it'll be a pretty penny. Won't mean anything to a man like that, of course. He must be rich as Croesus."

We were continuing in this vein when Reg walked in, looking cheerful but business-like.

"Oh, here you are, Harry," he said. "I was worried something had happened to you."

"To me? Why?"

"The police down the East End found a Chinese man lying an alley, wearing a very nice suit."

"Was he—?"

"Dead as a doornail. There were two wooden dowels stuck into his eye sockets," Reg said with relish.

"I don't understand," I said. "Yang's still in his room."

"No he ain't," said Reg. "They left his wallet on the body so people would know it wasn't a robbery, along with his papers. It was Yang — he gave you the slip. His Daimler was parked in the next street. That's why I thought you must have been with him."

Walker and I hurried up to Yang's room with Reg lumbering behind. The clerk knocked several times and called Yang's name. There was no reply, and after a minute, he opened the door with a passkey.

Of course, the room was empty. I remembered what Yang had said about discovering secrets of life and death and wondered if he had anticipated something like this.

It looked as though Yang had been getting ready to go back to China, with everything packed away and his luggage stacked up neatly. Just a few personal items remained: a set of tortoiseshell brushes on the dresser, a scarf tossed over the back of a chair. There was a cushion on the floor and a saucer but no sign of the cat. The window was shut, but the catch was open.

"Think Yang slipped out the window?" asked Reg.

"Must have done," says Walker. "He couldn't have got out of the building the back way. He would have been seen."

"I suppose he might have shinnied down the drainpipe," I said. It was hard to imagine Yang, in his spotless suit, engaged in anything so grubby. "I thought there were people keeping an eye out."

"Don't worry about it," said Reg, flipping open the top suitcase. Inside was a pile of neatly folded shirts. "Arthur won't mind. Yang's out of it now, and that's all he cared about."

Reg took a framed silver photograph of a pretty girl with bobbed hair out of a pocket in the suitcase. At first I thought she was an American movie starlet, until I saw that she was an Oriental. There was a tabby cat in her arms; even in black and white I recognised the animal with its piercing eyes.

Reg put the picture back and started opening other pockets in the suitcase, looking for valuables.

"You can't go rummaging through a hotel guest's property," said Walker. "Even a Chinese guest."

"What's it matter? He's dead now."

I shut the suitcase so quickly that Reg had to snatch his hands away.

He looked at me reproachfully. "Fill your pockets while you

can, Stubbs. You're out of a job now."

"How did you find out so quickly about Yang being killed?"

"I tipped the constabulary off about Yang a few days ago just as a precautionary measure."

"Did you tell Arthur about that?" I asked.

"What Arthur doesn't know won't hurt him. As soon as Yang's name came up, the police contacted me first thing. As a matter of fact, they asked me to officially identify the body."

"You?"

"Always happy to help the boys in blue." Reg smirked and pulled out a silver cigarette case with an Oriental design. "And pick up a keepsake."

"Did you get his watch, too?"

"It was only a cheap watch. Then I thought I'd come over here and have a look around before the police did."

"You've had your look around," said Walker. "Let's get back to reception before they show up."

We went back down, where Reg expounded his theory that Yang had arranged a rendezvous and the Triads had ambushed him.

"They got him good and proper. No torture. I reckon one man held him and the other one—fttt!" Reg made a gesture of sticking two fingers into my eyes. "The Triads cut up the body when they want to humiliate the victim—'lingchee,' that is—but that takes time..."

We were interrupted by the arrival of a pair of police constables. I recognised the PC who had attended the shooting incident, and he recognised me. He sent his colleague up with Walker to look at the room and addressed me politely.

"Am I correct in saying that you are a Mr Stubbs, lately employed to assist a Chinese gentleman?" There was no point in denying it. "Would you be so good as to accompany me to the station? I believe that you may be able to help us with our enquiries concerning the late Mr Yang."

I spent a few hours answering questions and making my statement. I described the encounter with the other Chinese as an argument rather than a fight, and omitted some other details such as Arthur's involvement, but gave them a broadly accurate outline. Not that the police were so very interested. Yang's murder did not cause much of a ripple anywhere. The detail of having his eyes poked out with wooden skewers was the one outstanding feature of the crime, but having played on that for what it was worth in terms of Oriental barbarism, the newspapers had nothing else to say on the matter. The prevailing view was that Yang was a gangster who was seeking to expand his gang's influence in the Chinese community in London and had fallen foul of the existing interests.

Or, if you believed the one anonymous Chinese shopkeeper the papers quoted, a group of right-thinking vigilantes had taken the law into their own hands and executed justice to keep the scourge of crime away from Limehouse.

The body was packed up and shipped out posthaste. The Chinese always send their dead back home for burial, wherever they die. Yang's baggage was whisked away, unmolested I trust, by some efficient agent.

Perhaps I was the only one in London to mourn him. I had become used to his odd ways, and I was ready to count Yang as a friend. As for his final encounter, I rather thought he deliberately slipped away so I would have no part in what he must have suspected would be a terminal matter. I took it as a favour and not a slight.

I thought occasionally of the girl with bobbed hair waiting for him in Shanghai, and whether I should write. Would Yang's employers inform her of his death, or would she still be waiting for him to return? Not that I had an address to write to, but I did think of her.

The police investigation was cursory. Having pegged it as a matter between Chinese, they felt no great need to explore further. An inspector from the Metropolitan Police made some remarks in the papers about the difficulties about investigating that sort of case. The Chinese legation said that the event was regrettable but showed no inclination to raise a hue and cry. The legation represented the new revolutionary Kuomintang government in Peking, while Shanghai was still under the sway of the old government of the Republic of China. They would not wish to draw attention to the incident and the rise of gangsterism in a city that they claimed but did not control.

"All's well that ends well," was Arthur's view.

The only loser was Reg, who had fallen from Arthur's favour. Looting from the dead was not respectful; talking to the police without getting leave doubly so.

"No wonder he has trouble sleeping at night," said Arthur. "Though I gather it was something you told him."

"What was?"

"He keeps getting nightmares about a Chinese strangler and wakes up choking." He tapped his temple. "Power of the mind. A guilty conscience is a dangerous thing, as I always say."

"We still have the question of Roslyn D'Onston," I said. "The purpose of Yang's visit was to establish if D'Onston was alive. I tend to the conclusion that the answer is in the affirmative."

Arthur has a mind like a steel trap and an eye for the angle that everyone else has missed. Powell's sudden death and Howard's wild claims might not amount to much. But Arthur has his own sources of information.

"That's a stretch," he said at last. "But people have some funny notions. If your Mrs Lavinia psychic does think she is Roslyn D'Onston, there might be some undesirable possibilities arising. We can't have her setting about our local ladies of the night with a straight razor, collecting ingredients for her witch's brew. Also... Yang's mob will want to do something about his being bumped off. Reg may be wide of the mark on some points, but he's right when he says they never forget a grudge."

"I'll talk to her," I said impulsively. "Either she's just an innocent old woman, or there is something in what Howard was saying and... well, I'll talk to her."

"You're forgetting something, aren't you, Stubbsy? Suppose Lavinia really is a Medusa who can kill you with a look." He gave a light snort. "You'd be struck as dead as Powell."

I had not really thought out the matter as far as that. "You think there's something in this evil-eye business?"

"Power of the mind," he said. "Some men die just because they think their number's up. You go talk to her, Stubbsy, but you take some protection from the evil eye."

"What, like a crucifix or something?"

"No Stubbsy, not like a ruddy crucifix. I respect the church as much as any man, but this is not in their line. This is more your white magic versus black magic sort of affair."

It occurred to me to mention my ring with the green star-stone, though I doubted it was the right sort of thing. And Arthur was well ahead of me.

"As luck would have it, I know a man who makes protective amulets for just that contingency." He placed a small object, wrapped in a scrap of cotton, on the table.

"What's this?"

"Open it." Arthur looked amused at my perplexity. "A little talisman from your friend and mine, Mr Whatley. Whatley's charms can do a sick man more good than three months in Baden-Baden. This one is guaranteed against the witch's curse, or your money back."

It was a blue stone the size and shape of a bean. There was a flaw or carving in it too small for me to see properly. Arthur's tone was bantering, but there was something behind it. He knew more than he was letting on. "Hold it in your hand when you talk to her, and you'll come to no harm. Mind you, Whatley reckons you've got no chance. He says her kind can hide in places ordinary people can't go."

"He helped you?"

He shrugged modestly. "You know me—I do business with all sorts."

Chapter Ten

The Breaking of the Circle

I had the back-door key to Maycot in my pocket. I could have entered like a thief, but there was really no need for subterfuge. I knocked on the front door like any respectable visitor. The curtains were drawn, leading me to wonder if a séance was in progress even though there was no meeting listed on the notice board.

I knocked again and listened. I heard no reply and no sound from within, nor was there any response to a third knock, which echoed throughout the house.

If there was nobody home, I would not have an interview with Lavinia. But since I had the means of entry, it might give me an opportunity to look around a little for clues. It was not quite the honest thing to do, but my role in the field of collections was sharpened by an understanding of the legal considerations: since I had a key, I was not breaking or forcing an entry or damaging property, and since I had no intention of removing anything from the premises, I could not be charged with burglary.

The back door led into the pantry, which in turn led into the kitchen. A cupboard door lay open, revealing shelves loaded with pots of flour, bottles of pickling vinegar, and jars of dried fruit. I skirted the open door and edged into the hallway. I opened each door as quietly as possible and stood listening. Perhaps the sitters at a séance would not be at liberty to come and answer the door even if they heard my knocking. There was not the slightest sound.

The Theosophy Circle's office was a side room off the drawing room. I opened the drawing room door with infinite caution and peered into the darkness beyond.

You know when something is not right the moment you get into a house, even if you don't know how you know. My instincts whispered that something was not right here. The table was laid out as if for a séance, the candlestick holder was in the centre, and there was something white on the dark tablecloth. But there were no people present, or so I thought when I entered the room.

"You."

I jumped at the voice, quiet as it was, coming from behind me. It took me a few moments to make out Lavinia. She was sitting back in an armchair as though exhausted. It was too dark to see her face, but I looked away anyway and clutched the blue pebble in my fist.

"I did knock on the door," I said.

"Oh," she said faintly. Then, after a pause, she said, "Could I trouble you for a glass of water? I'm afraid I'm not very well."

"May I turn the light on?"

"Certainly."

Lavinia was deathly pale, her skin contrasting all the more with a green velvet dress. She looked smaller and older. I had to help her with the glass. Her hand with the broken fingers was still bandaged, and she was terribly feeble. When she looked up, I looked away, wary of danger from those watery blue eyes.

On the dining table, in addition to the candelabra, was what looked like the skull of a goat and a sort of silver dagger. Thick lines of salt marked out a pentacle on the table.

"I'm afraid every time you see me I need medical attention," she said at last. "But don't call anyone just yet. Give me a minute."

"What happened here?"

"I made a terrible, terrible mistake." Her light manner dissolved suddenly, and she started sobbing quietly. Fat tears left trails down her powdered face. Eventually, she pulled herself together and gestured towards the drinks cabinet. "Please, a little sherry if you could."

It was locked, but under the circumstances, I felt justified in wrenching the door open. Such locks are decorative items to keep the servants out. Inside were two filled decanters and some delicate cut-glass sherry glasses. Careful not to turn my back or look directly at her, I filled one with the paler sherry and passed it to her. She sipped it eagerly and seemed to draw some strength.

"Victor," she started and stopped. "Victor is…"

I waited, but she did not continue.

"It was Howard," I said.

"Yes. No… the man who calls himself Howard now—he's gone mad. Utterly mad… no, that won't do. You know, don't you, about Roslyn D'Onston?"

"I know something about him," I said carefully.

"May I have another glass? Thank you. Please, take a seat, and I'll tell you the whole thing—whether you believe it or not. I'm done anyway." I refilled her glass. She took a long sip and then started up in a stronger voice.

"Howard, as you may know, joined us at the Theosophy Circle about a year ago. On the same day, the maid discovered a letter stuck between the floorboards addressed to 'One Who Shall Come After.' It was in code but signed by D'Onston. Victor couldn't make anything of it. Against my better judgement, I let Howard have it.

"Howard became utterly fascinated with the man. Read all of his dreadful works. You see, D'Onston was everything Howard wasn't. D'Onston was such a dashing fellow. A cavalry officer who had fought in wars. A man who had travelled the world when Howard only travelled through books. D'Onston had thrown himself into the practical side of the occult, he had been to Africa and India, seen miracles, and studied at the feet of masters. Howard tinkered about in his laboratory with test tubes.

"It impressed him also that D'Onston was very successful with women. Howard couldn't talk to one his own age without blushing and stammering. He decoded the letter, and he was convinced it was meant for him. He even hinted that D'Onston must have been his real father. He was besotted. Tried to copy his mannerisms."

"Even though D'Onston may have been Jack the Ripper?"

Lavinia sighed sadly. "That just added to his lure. Before the letter, Howard had been very much the dilettante, toying with his experiments, but he started working like a demon—in his cellar laboratory at all hours of day and night. He spent a fortune on old manuscripts and original copies of obscure works—not to mention chemicals and equipment. It's nice for a man to have an interest that keeps him occupied, but he had become secretive.

"Of course, we knew he was up to something. Victor put the fear of God into one of Howard's servants, and the man told us that two men had brought a coffin one night and carried it down to the laboratory. It was supposed to be secret, but you can't keep anything from servants…

"Howard was attempting Palingenesis on a human being. He reduced the body to its essential salts and used the art to call up a life-sized phantom inside a giant glass jar."

"Good God," I said.

"At first he was using a charcoal burner to apply heat, but he could only get the phantom to form for a few seconds at a time. But that was where Howard was cleverer than the ancients. He mixed in radium salts that provided a steady heat, distributed evenly—and he stabilized the phantom so it could survive hours at a time in its glass prison.

"We had to put a stop to it. Victor and I confronted him. He caved in and promised to end it, and we thought he had. We should not have taken his word…

"Howard disappeared for a few days, and when we saw him again, he was different. That was just before you came. He was more secretive but lively. He hardly said anything, but he had a sparkle in his eye and seemed to be… laughing at us. Howard was not the laughing sort."

"As though his personality had altered," I said.

"Then this Mr Yang turned up — Victor was so frightened of him! Because of the opium business."

"What business?"

"Victor's province is one of the ones where they still grow opium for the China trade. When he heard Yang was from

Shanghai, he expected some unpleasantness... he was in such a tizzy. And there was that terrible séance, and Elizabeth being so ill... we were all so busy with everything, and Howard disappeared for good. His servants say he just packed up one night and left with one case. He'd been spending more and more time out of the house... somewhere. Victor went to the laboratory, but it had been stripped. Could I possibly have another glass?"

I refilled it silently.

"Howard came back today. Now he is convinced he is Roslyn D'Onston. He was terribly elated that Yang was dead. He said the Chinese had come for him, and he'd fooled them into murdering each other. He wants to complete his work..."

The sherry, combined with the aftermath of her ordeal, was beginning to have an effect. She trailed off, and I had to prompt her to go on. "His work?"

"Palingenesis. From phantom to flesh, shadow to substance. Give it a little blood, and it survives longer. Well, we've always known that from Hartmann's work on vampires. Howard has weaned it from blood to solid meat—following Paracelsus' theory, I suspect—and it doesn't fade at all. He's as happy as a boy with how it's grown, except for one thing. Animal flesh is not enough. It warps; the Palingenesis needs human flesh. A special flesh, like in the old days—the sacred sacrifice. That's why he came back."

She looked me in the face, and this time I did not turn away.

"He thought that Victor and I had some book or teaching that we wouldn't share with him. I tried to tell him that Theosophy is a purely scientific discipline; we have no secrets... it's funny, really, because before, Howard was adamant in his scientism. Now he's full of mumbo jumbo. We argued, and he... attacked me. When I came round, I heard them in the office." She nodded at the door to the little side room. "He was trying to get Victor to talk. Torturing him."

I started up, but she gestured weakly for me to sit down. "Don't go in there. I'm quite sure Victor was dead by the time Howard left. You can't help him. I saw... please don't go in there."

I looked anxiously at the door.

"Victor couldn't tell him anything because he had nothing to tell… but it went on and on. I prayed for it to be over. The oddest thing was before he left, Howard laid out those things on the table, those… black-magic stage props."

I suspected there would be an anonymous letter to the newspaper explaining how the Theosophy Circle had descended to Satanism and explaining it all. That was the killer's modus operandi, as the police call it.

"And you don't know where he's gone?"

"I'm afraid not."

"I'll telephone for a doctor," I said. "But I do have to look in the other room."

"Please… all I ever wanted was for Victor to be happy. That's why I took up this whole Theosophy thing… I just wanted a garden…" She broke down into sobbing again.

I opened the door. I did not know what I was expecting. Perhaps the wooden skewers that Yang had suffered made me unconsciously expect that Victor would be a human pincushion.

It had not occurred to me that D'Onston was a completely cold-blooded individual for whom the Whitechapel killings were simple medical procedures. Nor had I appreciated that not all the stories of his magic powers over the human body were exaggerations.

I would never have recognised Victor but for the mouth. The mouth had been left intact so that his torturer could extract information. Enough of him was left that he must have retained his power of speech until the end. When we talk of someone being torn apart or ripped to shreds, it is a figure of speech. In this case, the description was approximately correct.

The only thing I will note about that scene, and which still haunts me, was something lying on the desk on top of some papers, next to an inkstand and an ashtray. It was a pale thing that might at first sight have been a discarded cuff. It took me a moment to recognise it.

It was one of Victor's hands.

There was no blood; it had been detached easily as one unscrews a fitting. As I gazed in horrified fascination, the hand gave a single twitch, like a spider with a broken back, and was still again.

I left, shutting the door, shutting the image out of my mind—and trying not to think of what soft thing I had trodden on when I entered.

Chapter Eleven

The Reanimation of Robert D'Onston Stephenson

How could I find the lair of a man who had deliberately hidden himself? He might have been anywhere in London. Except that I did not think he had travelled very far, not under the circumstances. He had most likely gone to ground somewhere close by so that he could come and go easily.

I did have one clue to go by. Lavinia, who was now in the care of the doctor, told me that Howard was feeding the reconstituted body quantities of red meat to give it substance. Assuming that the usual principles apply, to build up a twelve-stone man, you would need—at the very least—the same weight in meat over just a few weeks. Perhaps you would need several times that amount. I know for a fact it requires more than a stone of scraps to get a pig to put on a stone. Somebody would have started ordering meat in large quantities in the few weeks before I began my search.

It was late at night, but I still had the key to my father's shop. I knew where he kept his order book. There was no need to disturb him at that hour. I spent a few minutes going through that ledger, reading the careful handwriting, watching the march of days, and feeling a glow as I met so many familiar names. I saw the addresses of houses where I had made deliveries on my bicycle. There were little marks to show who liked their steak cut thick or chops trimmed lean and who would want him to throw in a bag of scraps for the dog.

Along with the names I recognized, there was a stranger.

Mr Smith paid cash on the nail and had deliveries four times a week. He was ordering ten pounds at a time of what are known in the trade as broken meats—offcuts, which usually ended up in sausages or the mincer, but he took them on the bone. The first address was, of course, Howard's. After that, the deliveries went to a different set of premises. The last one included a request for a sheep's head.

And so I found myself walking down the deserted streets to an address in South Norwood as the hour approached midnight. My hobnail boots, the ones I wore when there might be doors to be broken down, sounded like a carthorse coming down the road.

In case you should get the wrong idea, I was not going because I was brave and fearless. Arthur had joked about me, thinking I was Douglas Fairbanks after the Shackleton affair, and perhaps it had sharpened my appetite for adventure. But there was nothing heroic about what I was doing now.

After the fight with the Chinese strangler, I had started wondering if I had lost my nerve. I had lost two bouts in the boxing ring, but they never shook my faith the way the fight with the strangler had.

I had been glad to get out of that encounter in one piece—but, as they say, once bitten, twice shy.

I went on not because I was brave but because I was afraid. As a fighter, if you don't face up to your fears, you're nothing. It's that willingness to stand up and punch and be punched that makes you what you are. I could not let that be taken away from me. I am not nothing. I will not walk away from a fight.

So even though I felt my stomach fluttering unsteadily, even though my mouth was dry, I kept going. My hands were thrust in my coat pockets. In one pocket was the charm from Whatley; in the other was a pair of knuckle-dusters. I had contemplated other weapons, but they might be too conspicuous on a man walking after midnight.

It seemed that I was walking against some resistance, as though the level street was actually uphill. The streetlights flickered more than usual, and the shadows crowded round more densely. I knew it was all in my head. But I wondered if someone had put it there.

I pushed on, and I felt a prickling on the back of my neck. I sensed that I was not alone. I turned, and there was a cat, walking twenty paces behind me—a big tabby cat. I stopped, and the cat stopped. It was not the usual mackerel tabby but more of a marbled pattern. It sat down, looked at me, and gave a long, slow blink with emerald green eyes.

"If you've come to help, Mister Pussycat, you're very welcome," I said in an undertone. "Maybe you've the same score to settle as me."

I started walking again, and without looking back, I knew the cat was still following.

Turning back was no longer a possibility—not with someone watching, even if it was only a cat. I set my jaw and pushed on until the resistance melted away. The tightness around my chest loosened, and I turned off the main road on to the street noted in my father's ledger.

A minute later, I arrived at a small, circular structure with glazed bricks and red tiles. It was off Brickyard Street where there are so many manufacturing firms. The building had a neglected air about it, but faint light shone through a frosted side window.

My path had taken me over dead bodies, through a thicket of lies and misdirection. I had defied the attempts to throw me off the road. Finally, as the poet Mr Robert Browning might have said, Childe Harry to the dark tower came.

The cat stopped two paces behind me. There was no bell or door knocker, so I gave a peremptory rap as I would for a defaulting debtor. I listened and knocked again. No reply.

I kicked squarely at the height of the lock. The hinges must have been rusted because they gave way along with the dead bolt. The whole thing toppled inwards with an empty boom.

Inside, there was no sign of life except for an oil lantern hanging from a hook. The building consisted of a single, medium-sized room, the centre of which was occupied by a low platform of brick. It was a workshop with a solid chimney for a furnace or oven, a high ceiling, and beams overhead.

I went looking for entrances to concealed tunnels and found

nothing. The bare stone floor was flat and smooth. There was not the least sign of a hairline crack to give away an opening. There were no currents of air and no spots that sounded hollow. I spent fifteen minutes searching in this fashion.

The room was not large, and I had circled it three times when the cat came in. It walked to one side of the brick platform, sat down, and wrapped its tail round its feet. The cat gave a single, low meow, the way cats do when they wish a door to be opened for them.

"What do you want?" I stopped dead.

The cat was sitting in front of a round iron manhole cover. I could not have failed to see it before.

I had walked over that exact spot not a minute previously, and I would swear on a Bible that the manhole had not been there earlier. But there it was, as real and solid as anything.

It was not too hard to lever it open with a piece of scrap metal. Below was a sheer cylindrical drop of ten feet. Iron rungs driven into the brick walls made a ladder. I unhooked the oil lantern and lowered myself, watched by the cat. The first few feet of bricks were crude and uneven. After that, they were flat and red like the old Roman bricks in London Wall.

This truly was a descent into madness. I have never suffered from that morbid terror of confined spaces known as claustrophobia, but when I reached the bottom rung and saw that the manhole was invisible above me, I felt something very like it.

I was in a narrow corridor with an arched ceiling and damp stone walls—old stone, I could tell. The floor was worn into a channel from who knew how many centuries of walking feet.

"Meredith, we're in," I whispered to myself, as though the old joke was a protective spell.

A faint light glimmered ahead from another oil lantern such as the one I held. I walked towards it.

After thirty feet, the corridor opened into a roughly circular chamber with arched entranceways leading into darkness.

One side was a sort of study with a folding table and a single wooden chair with a coat over the back of it. All around were piles of books with places marked in them with slips of paper.

There was an oil lamp on a hook, and a lit candle on the table. I felt the seat of the chair and found it warm.

In the middle of the room was a circular stone wall ten or twelve feet across and a foot high, studded with stone posts; it opened into a pit below. A wooden ladder was propped up beside it. There was not a single sound.

"Mr D'Onston," I said in as firm a voice as I could manage—my debt-collecting voice. "Or rather, Mr Robert D'Onston Stephenson. I might call you Howard Phillips. though you've no right to the name."

I expected him to step out of the shadows at any moment but saw nothing but a slight movement down in the pit. I wondered again if I might have come too late.

"You should properly be dead. You've no right still to be walking this Earth and certainly not in a body stolen from another man—a foolish young man, whose only crime was that he was too easily entranced by your stories. Your lies, in fact. He brought you back from the dead. You repaid him by tricking him into an exchange of bodies."

I had put down the oil lamp and was moving around stealthily as I spoke, my words echoing between the stone walls. The blue charm was clutched in my fist.

"You were convincing enough as long as you kept your mouth shut. But I don't think you know a tenth as much about Palingenesis as Howard, and it showed. Also, you talked about what Yeats and Madame Blavatsky talked about in Maycot as though you were there. And when you came to talk to me in the pub, I saw through you in a minute."

I had hoped that I could goad him into revealing himself. Roslyn was an arrogant man and not one to stay silent when he was being attacked. I peeked through one of the arches and saw the gleam of glassware.

"Now you're tired of being him. You don't like being a short, pudgy man with weak eyes. You want to be yourself again. But Howard was an amateur and made a botched job of restoring your carcass, so you want to put it right."

I was not sure whether it was a trick of the dim light, but some of the walls seemed to be carved with reliefs of grotesque figures, somewhere between human and animal. The shadows were distracting, but I kept focused, looking and listening for the slightest movement.

"You tried to kill Yang at the séance, but you bungled that one."

"Help."

The high-pitched voice was faint and tremulous but unmistakable. It came from the pit, of course.

After looking over my shoulder in both directions, I heaved the rickety old ladder and lowered it into the pit. I could not see inside until I brought an oil lamp over. The drop was about ten feet, and what I had taken for a pit was in fact an opening onto another level below with more arched doorways leading away from a central chamber. The ground was littered with bones, mainly mutton and beef with some pork. The place had that familiar butcher smell of meat and blood. The only other object of note was an earthenware bowl full of water, like a dog bowl. Oddly, there were no flies.

I took the ladder steps carefully. They were unsteady, and I half expected the rungs to give way under my weight. I stopped after each step, looking up and down, ready for an attack at any moment. None came, and I stepped onto the stone floor. Still moving slowly, I picked up the ladder and lay it on its side. I did not want someone hauling it up from above and leaving me down here.

Watching me with wide eyes was little Chun Hua, the Chinese Spring Flower.

Roslyn wanted human flesh and blood to restore his corpse to full humanity, and not from just any source. No, he had gone back to the oldest requirement of all: he had to have the blood of a virgin princess. Chun Hua was that "necessary element for a successful outcome" in the letter that Yang's people had intercepted and that had so alarmed the Wu brothers.

Chun Hua's hands were tied above her head. The cord passed through a hole cut through a stone protuberance. As though it had been made for sacrificial victims when chamber was sculpted out of the bedrock.

"Don't worry," I said in a low voice, swinging the lantern

around as I looked in all directions. "I'm here now."

"Shhh," she warned.

The bones on the floor were well chewed and picked clean of meat, and there were a lot of them.

Looking over my shoulder, I pulled at the ends of the cord that bound Chun Hua. After some resistance, it came free. It was a long cord, perhaps a washing line. She stepped away, rubbing her wrists. She did not seem to have been harmed.

"Are you hurt?"

She shook her head. I led her back to where I had descended, and I stood the ladder up again. Chun Hua did not climb it but suddenly pointed past me into the darkness. Something moved, far back in the shadows, scuffling on the stone floor.

"Howard?" I asked tentatively. "My name is Harry Stubbs."

There was no reply, but I sensed I was being watched from the darkness.

"I know what you have suffered. I mean you no harm."

My plan, such as it was, involved catching D'Onston and compelling him to return Howard to his proper body while D'Onston reoccupied his own resurrected remains. I had assumed that Howard would be a willing participant in this operation.

I put the lantern down slowly. "I've come to help."

Even as he approached from out of the murk, well before I could see him clearly, I wondered whether I had misjudged the situation. He moved more like a panther prowling towards a tethered goat than a friend, and in the last two steps, when the lamplight caught him, I knew that everything was wrong.

I don't know anything about the inner workings of Palingenesis or what had caused it to go so far wrong. The lamp revealed an enormous, shambling figure that looked like a reflection in a fairground mirror or a distorted human shape seen through wavy glass. He was more a monster than a man. But at first, the only things that struck me about him were the size of him and, as I saw his face, the utter insanity in those eyes.

There was no reason, no sense, no spark of human recognition—only the look, perhaps, of a starving man presented with a plate of roast beef. With an inarticulate cry, he reached out for Chun Hua with one misshapen hand.

After that, things happened quickly. My recollections are a collage of vivid fragments that I have pieced together as best I may. What follows would not satisfy any serious commentator on the art of pugilism, but it is the most accurate I can manage.

Chun Hua screamed shrilly. I took hold of the monster's wrist—as thick as my biceps—as he reached for her, and I pushed it away.

He was so focused on the girl that he had hardly noticed me. It took him a second to react. If I had been quicker, I might have done something more decisive at that moment, but I still had hopes of avoiding a fight.

He struck at me with his other hand; I blocked it. He inexpertly flailed, breaking my grip on his wrist, and we sprang apart. We squared up to each other. The monster focused on me for the first time; the two halves of his face did not seem to join up properly. He peeled his lips back in a snarl, revealing too-big teeth.

He was big, the biggest I ever fought. When he stepped forward, I was in his shadow, and it was like having a storm cloud towering over me. It was not his size, though, but his jerky, insect-like movements and his horrible parody of a human form that sent cold fear through me. I slipped my hands quickly into the knuckle-dusters.

He was not in any sort of defensive posture, and I loosed a straight left to his midsection. The monster just let out a little huff, and that was all. It was like punching the heavy bag, or a side of beef; his flesh was that unyielding. I had my first inkling that, contrary to appearances, this was not a living thing. He was animated by some force other than normal vitality, and it would take more than usual effort to knock him down.

He moved as smartly as a living man, though, and when he hit me back with his oversized fist, the blow caught my shoulder. The force of the impact almost overbalanced me.

I skipped back, and his next two blows stirred the air. I moved better than most boxers my size, and there was plenty of room for me to circle round and keep away as the monster tried to close to striking distance.

The knuckle-duster is a much-misunderstood item of weaponry. To the uninitiated, it is just a set of brass rings that you wear over your fingers, and the popular belief is that all the effect comes from striking your opponent with metal rather than bare knuckles. If that were really the case, you'd break your fingers when you used them.

Real brass knuckles have a T-shaped extension that fits snugly into your palm, transferring the force of the blow into your hand rather than your fingers. You can hit much harder than you can with unprotected fingers.

In addition, a knuckle-duster gives weight to the blow. Weighted gloves are a notorious topic in boxing circles. I've sat through many an argument about whether Jack Dempsey had plaster of Paris on his hands when he won the title in '19 or, even more improbably, had an iron spike inside his glove. Even the extra few ounces of a little plaster make a big difference. With a pair of solid twelve-ounce brass knuckle-dusters, I could take on Jack Dempsey or any other boxer with padded gloves. They are classed as a deadly weapon and rightly so.

After the incident with the Chinese wrestler, I had carried them and had practiced using them a couple of times. That saved my life in the underground chamber. The monster came forward, both hands stretched out towards me. In the poor light, I couldn't judge distance accurately. I did not stop to consider that one false move would see me dead. I stepped in and delivered a combination, left-right-left-right, against his chest and abdomen. One blow was fouled by his arm, but the others all connected with the solid thud of a sledgehammer on wood.

I fell back as one hand right hand caught hold of my coat. He pulled me into a clumsy but extraordinarily powerful left hook. It was like being hit by a tram, and I momentarily lost consciousness. Luckily, the coat tore as I fell backwards; otherwise, he would have kept hitting me, and that would have been the end of Harry Stubbs.

I stumbled back into the wall but somehow kept my feet. I did not know where I was or what was happening, but I knew

I was in a fight, and I could see enough to throw out the next combination, high and low.

His mouth was open, and white fragments showered from his teeth where the metal had struck. His head went back—as well it might; the blow was strong enough to crack the skull of any normal human—and I pressed on with a series of simple jabs, left or right, to get through whatever guard he had.

A pale shape moved upwards at the edge of my vision—Chun Hua disappearing over the top of the ladder. The monster kept pressing forward, and I had to keep circling around until I found myself cornered and had to back through an archway into pitch darkness. The only light was from the archway. From the echoes of my hobnail boots on the stone floor, I knew it was a spacious chamber, but my only concern was to get past the thing and back to the pit.

The absence of light did not trouble the thing I was fighting, and he moved directly towards me. In the deep gloom, I saw that his skin was faintly phosphorescent like a corpse glow or the light from a radium clock face.

He was not so light on his feet, and when I feinted left and darted right, he was wrong-footed enough for me to slip past like a schoolboy evading a clumsy beadle.

I dashed through to the pit, but I doubted I had enough lead to get up the ladder before he grabbed at my ankles. Instead of climbing, I turned and, in a moment of inspiration, dropped low as he rushed towards me.

I caught him low about the waist and, using his own momentum and my strength, heaved him up and over, not as neatly as the wrestler had thrown me but just as effectively. He crashed down like the proverbial ton of bricks. Unlike the wrestler, I was ready to take advantage when he landed with one arm outstretched. I jumped on his elbow, full force with both feet and all my weight and with the stone floor beneath. Going for the weak points. The impact would have snapped the arm of a living man like a dry stick, but the monster barely reacted.

As he raised himself on his other arm, I gave his head a mighty kick that laid him flat. Hoping it would take him a minute to recover, I turned to the ladder.

The ladder was gone. I was trapped with the monster.

I looked left and right, thinking I had got turned around, but the ladder had been pulled up.

The monster was stirring, heaving himself into a sitting position. I stepped over and gave him a roundhouse punch that would have embarrassed my trainer but was just the thing against a dazed opponent, and it put him back down again. Knuckle-duster notwithstanding, the blow left my hand singing.

He would not stay down for long. Nothing I could do would inflict any real damage on the thing. With a decent cleaver, I might have been able to do more, but not with bare hands.

The ladder was gone, but the length of cord that had bound Chun Hua was still there, at least twelve feet of it. The pit was barely ten feet deep. Doubling the cord over, I took the best run up I could, and, jumping high, succeeded in looping it over one of the balustrades above. I dangled for a second, my feet a foot above the ground, then awkwardly hauled myself up.

As I did so, I was all too aware that D'Onston was above me, the monster was below me, and there was no telling which was more dangerous. My main preoccupation was stopping the doubled rope from slipping through my fingers and wondering how high I was above the ground.

Behind and below me, the animate corpse gave a howl—and I felt his hand tighten on my foot and drag me down. The cord tightened like a bowstring.

The next thing I knew, my foot had slipped out of the boot, and I was scrambling upwards like a monkey up a palm tree, pulling myself onto the floor at the upper level while the monster howled behind me.

Chun Hua stood there in her white dress; then I saw that she was being held. Howard had her two wrists firmly in one hand. He looked down at me with amused contempt.

"May I ask how you discovered my retreat?" he asked.

"It's a long story," I said, getting up slowly, a little battered and awkward on one bare foot, but sound enough. I felt for the charm Arthur had given me and realised I had dropped it somewhere in the pit.

He looked at me.

The human gaze is a funny thing. You can feel the pressure of it when someone is watching you, even from behind. There is a certain electricity when you look into another's eyes. My belief is that the evil eye is nothing but an extension of the same effect, a sort of sympathetic influence turned bad. It crosses the gulf between individuals and allows the mind of one to wreak havoc on the body of another.

Looking into D'Onston's eyes was like looking up at the mouth of a well as I fell slowly down it, gently as thistledown. At the same time, I felt myself exhaling forcefully through no volition of my own, as though my breath was propelling me away, and all my vitality was flowing out into the air.

I did not have a clue how to fight it. I tried to wave my arms, move my legs, turn my head away, but I was completely disconnected from my own body. D'Onston had charge of the whole engine, and he knew the way to shut it down. If only I could shut my eyes or will myself blind to cut off that stare.

I focused my willpower, my determination, my whole strength into trying to reverse my fall. My descent may have slowed a little, but the world continued to grow ever more distant. My breath was all gone, and now I heard the rush of blood in my ears and the thud-thud-thud of my heartbeat slowing down, slowing down.

It was infuriating that this pudgy little man was standing a few feet away, just out of my reach, and I could do nothing. I could see him exerting his will, and the strain was starting to show on him.

The pressure on me eased. I felt myself drifting back upwards towards the world, and I took half a breath before D'Onston redoubled his effort again, and I was resubmerged in the void, drowning slowly. I was proving hard to kill, no doubt a much tougher specimen than Powell but still no match for D'Onston.

Even the toughest chicken gets its neck wrung if you twist hard enough, and D'Onston could twist very hard indeed. My heart went thud... thud... thud... then missed a beat.

I must have blacked out because when I came to, I was

panting heavily, gasping in great lungfuls of air. Someone was standing between me and D'Onston, blocking his line of sight, cutting off the lethal beam of his gorgon stare. I was looking at the back of an immaculately tailored, oyster-grey, raw-silk suit. Mr Yang was facing D'Onston.

"The Si Fan cannot be flouted with impunity," Yang said. "You can never escape."

"If the Divine King in Yellow's cohorts can't kill you, I certainly can," said D'Onston, unperturbed. "Call yourself a Taoist adept, eh?"

D'Onston raised a hand. I am certain the words he spoke next would have paralysed Yang or done some other mischief—had not Yang coolly shot him in the chest three times before he could get the words out. Chun Hua flinched as the bullets passed inches over her head.

"Taoist magic," Yang murmured as the echo of the shots died away.

D'Onston looked shocked. Then his face gradually twisted. It was an expression of pain but also in a transfiguration, as when an actor steps out of one role and takes up another, adjusting his features to the character he is playing. The new actor looked about in confusion and dismay, not understanding what had happened to him, before taking half a step and toppling to the ground.

Yang had fired at D'Onston; but when the body died, it was occupied by Howard. Yang confirmed that the man was dead. Chun Hua was shaking and clung on to my hand for dear life but was unscathed.

Mocking laughter sounded from the pit beneath us.

"The situation is not necessarily to our advantage." Yang gestured me over to the deal table, where a book lay open beside an oil lamp, and pointed to the place. "We must be quick. Can you read this?"

"I don't understand."

"Read me the words here, by the dragon-tail symbol."

I leaned close, trying to make out the writing. At first it looked as if it was in a foreign alphabet, but I gradually made out an old-fashioned script where the letters flowed together.

"It's not proper words, "I said. "This one looks like—'thro-dog'?"

A low tone, deep as an organ pipe, sounded in the chamber, echoing and re-echoing as though through many caverns farther below us. Then it arose again on a slightly different note. Chun Hua let out a shriek as the face of the thing from the pit appeared over the edge. Yang shot at him, and I believe he hit several times, but the bullets had no more effect than a peashooter.

As the monster pulled himself fully up to our level, I disengaged from Chun Hua's hold. The knuckle-duster was still on my left hand, and as he rose, I punched the monster square in the face, sending him tumbling back into darkness.

I peered down, trying to see through the gloom, and saw him rising up on the other side. I could not fathom how he was climbing that sheer surface. I went round to tackle him, but the monster had already achieved the stone floor and adopted a fighting stance. When I closed, he threw a straight right at me, which I dodged.

The thing looked quite different now that D'Onston occupied the body. His face was a grisly mask of cunning and malice. Howard had never boxed in his life, but D'Onston held his guard like a decent amateur and knew how to use his reach. His blows were inexpert but dangerous.

My right hand was less useful without the weight and power of a knuckle-duster, making me a one-armed fighter. He was one armed too, but his left elbow was not as badly damaged as I'd expected—as though it was healing even as we fought. His attacks were not frenzied but deliberate. After being confined to the short, dumpy frame of Howard, D'Onston was revelling in the power and strength of his regenerated body.

I was aware of the booming from the pit, rumbling and rolling. Some corner of my mind registered the fact that the sounds were resolving themselves into words. And the rhythm of it... was the same as in the séance. But a thousand times stronger.

Movement was my only means of survival, and I used the space as best I could to avoid his blows while trying to maneuver him around. He followed me, pressing closely. I tried a left hook, angling to knock him back into the pit. My blow staggered him, but his counterpunch knocked me down.

D'Onston ignored me and loped towards Yang—who, unable to read himself, held the book up for Chun Hua. She was reading haltingly, following the words with a finger. As D'Onston closed on them, Yang shouted out a string of words she had deciphered.

Like a sandcastle kicked over by a bully, or a snowball struck by a cricket bat, the monster disintegrated into fine particles. There was nothing left but a cloud of grey dust settling to the ground. Those words had somehow unbound the atoms that had been bound together by Palingenesis.

Dust to dust: the mortal remains of Robert D'Onston Stephenson, falling like featherdown from a burst pillow.

"Was he just a bad dream?" Chun Hua asked me, looking wonderingly.

"A dead man who dreamed he was alive," said Yang. "Until we woke him."

The booming from the pit had faded into a single mournful note. Then, the drumming started up again, quickly becoming louder. Whatever D'Onston had called on had passed through some veil, and it was still rising from the deep.

"Come now," said Yang as I goggled at the cloud. He took the oil lamp in one hand and Chun Hua by the other and hurried back to the corridor. I followed, the stone flags cold under my one bare foot.

As soon as we reached the surface, Yang instructed me to replace the manhole cover. I saw that there was another light, flickering in many colours, which was blotted out when I closed the lid. Even with the cover down, I could hear the bass voice rumbling and feel the vibration through the ground. While I was staring at it, Yang tugged my sleeve and ushered me outside with Chun Hua.

"What is it?" I asked. "How can we stop it?"

Yang shook his head. I recalled how the formless ectoplasm had reached for him, and for some reason I thought of an earthquake of boiling mud.

As soon as we were outside he placed his hands against

the wall. "Heaven and Earth are without limit." Yang looked as though he was trying to push the wall over.

"Can I help?"

"Please stand back."

It was a physical impossibility to push a wall over. But that wasn't quite what he was trying to do. It was more as if he was shaping the vibration that was coming up from below, channelling it with tiny movements of his hands. There was no sign of strain on his face; Yang was as serene as if he always leaned against walls that way.

The sound grew louder, a thrumming note that I felt all the way through my chest, like a locomotive passing inches away.

They say a singer can shatter a wine glass with a high-pitched note, though I've never seen it done. Perhaps a similar effect occurred when, just for a moment, the solid wall wobbled like cardboard under Yang's hands, and the next second, the vibration rippled through it, and the whole building tumbled like a house of cards, collapsing in on itself with an oddly muted rumble. It was not an explosion but an implosion. The building just seemed to decide not to want to stand anymore and slumped into a compact heap with hardly any dust.

Then it was quiet again. There was no sound from under the ground. Yang turned to see Chun Hua and me gaping at him. He replaced his hat and flicked dust off his lapels. A tabby cat rubbed round his ankles. Yang petted it distractedly, saying something in Chinese.

I was forced to consider my own appearance: torn jacket, buttons gone from my shirt where I had scrambled out of the pit, face bloodied and bruised, one shoe missing. I removed the knuckle-duster from my left hand and wiped my face with a handkerchief.

"It is inconvenient for the Si Fan for you, who know so much, still to be alive," Yang told me.

I was looking down the barrel of his pistol. But I could tell now that this was merely a formality, like the cups of tea poured by the Wu brothers.

"I will report your death to my superiors," he said, putting the weapon away. "Just as you reported my death to the authorities."

"That was Reg Brown who identified the body for the police," I said. "Wrongly. Who was the it—the man I rescued you from?"

"He pierced me with two *chuan*; I returned them to him. The Si Fan are not attacked with impunity."

"And you gave him your suit and your papers so D'Onston would think you were dead. Then you used me to lure out D'Onston so you could get a shot at him."

"Indeed," he said.

"But you did save my life."

"No doubt you would have survived without my assistance," he said smoothly. "I apologise for interfering. However—if we do meet again, I warn you that it may be necessary to kill you."

"Oh," I said.

"Now, as you have been of such assistance, I will answer one of your questions."

I did not know what question to ask; there were so many. But Yang had already decided.

"Make your fist like this."

I followed his direction, holding my fist at waist level, thumb outwards.

"Strike like this." Yang extended his arm, exhaling and rotating his fist as he did so. I copied the action, repeating it several times under his direction. "Focus your energy. Concentrate on the fist."

It was an unfamiliar move, quite unlike the Western style but not altogether strange. There was something natural about it, as if my muscles were already tuned to it. It was like going back to a movement that I had known as a child but had forgotten.

"You must never share this knowledge with anyone," said Yang. "But if you practice one thousand times a day, one day you may break stones. Yes. Now, do it three times more, exactly like that."

I repeated the move as directed, wondering at now easy it felt. When I looked up again, Yang had disappeared.

"Can I go home now?" asked Chun Hua.

I walked half a mile with her, discarding my one shoe at an early stage. Walking on the pavement in stockinged feet is not a pleasant experience. She was exhausted. I had to carry her the next mile until we reached Brixton Hill, where I was able to flag down a cab. I had not formulated an explanation as to why I was accompanying a small Chinese girl, and the driver looked doubtful about taking us at first, but then his face lit up.

"Here—ain't you Harry Stubbs, the boxer?"

"As a matter of fact, I am."

"Well, I never! Hop in, Harry. I saw you fight Davy Berg at the Winter Gardens three years back."

The cabbie was a keen follower of the sport. He was less interested in why I was escorting Chun Hua than in reliving my contest against Davy Berg and why I let him get up in the third round, and soliciting my views on the current state of the fight game with particular reference to Frank Goddard's prospects for holding on to the title. Another man might have thought of contacting the National Society for the Prevention of Cruelty to Children; the cabbie was more interested in what I thought of the colour bar and whether rumours of my return to the game were well founded.

The cabbie was well-informed, firing off questions and opinions at a rapid pace. I worked hard to keep up while Chun Hua dozed next to me.

There was light at the windows of the Wu house, and the door opened as soon as the cab drew up. Most of the family spilled out onto the street to greet us. Yang must have apprised them of their daughter's rescue. I remained just long enough to see Chun Hua reunited with her tearful mother. Her father wanted to get on his knees in front of me, but I was having none of it. I stepped back into the cab and ordered the driver back to Norwood. The return of their daughter was more important to the Wu family than anything else. And it had been a long day.

When I finally reached home and escaped the friendly interrogation of my driver, a little ditty was going round my head. It was the final verse of Kipling's famous poem about East and West not meeting—the lines that Reg never got to:

"But there's neither East nor West
Nor border, breed nor birth
When two strong men meet face to face
Though they come from the ends of the Earth."

Epilogue

Breakfast at the Electric Café

Not long after these events, I was having breakfast at the Electric Café with Arthur at his special invitation. I had already given him a brief summary of the foregoing events, but now he was between consignments and wanted to hear the whole thing from start to finish.

He listened to my account without demur, methodically working his way through a Full English, cutting up his bacon, sausage, egg, tomato and mushroom into small pieces, hardly stopping me to ask a question. Listening to myself telling it, I was more incredulous than he was. It sounded in my ears like a mishmash of Frankenstein's monster, Count Dracula, and Jekyll and Hyde. Arthur took it all in with no appearance of concern.

"And that explains your casual appearance, Stubbsy," he said at the end, as though that was the mystery he wanted solving. He was referring to my old jacket, and the cap I was wearing in place of my missing bowler.

"My wardrobe is undergoing renewal." I had refused payment from Chun Hua's family, but a round little Chinese tailor had turned up at my lodgings a day later. He insisted on measuring me up for a list of missing or damaged items, namely "one gentleman's suit, one pair shoes, one bowler hat." The tailor was a cheerful, busy man who laughed at his difficulty in reaching around my chest and assured me that he would make me a suit in the latest style, soliciting my views on whether double-breasted would be best for my build.

"I will return for fitting next week," he beamed as he

finished. "Also, I will include three first-class gentlemen's shirts and three ties to go with suit. Necessary to have with a good suit."

"Thank you. Pass my thanks on to the Wu brothers."

"No, no, no!" he said, still smiling. "Not from any of the Mr Wu. This suit is complimentary on the special orders of Mr Henry Yang." He spoke the name reverently.

I had only ever worn ready-made suits, which were never quite a satisfactory fit on my physique. I would have been doubtful of a Chinese tailor before, but as this man had Yang's seal of approval, I looked forward to being the best-dressed man in Norwood.

Henry Yang, the tailor had called him. I never knew his name was the same as mine. I don't know why he never mentioned it.

"What you need to do now is to write the whole thing down from beginning to end," Arthur was saying. "Just as you've told me, minus a few incriminating details. Once you've got it all straight, make a fair copy in your best office handwriting."

"But I've already told you everything."

"I know you have. And a few others have told me a few things. Like who dug up Bill McCann's grave and what other grave they dug up a week later. Also, I can tell you that there's nothing under that workshop that collapsed—I had a couple of lads try it with pickaxes. Solid all the way down, and no sign of a manhole anywhere."

"I was there," I protested.

Arthur shrugged, and hinted that I might have been hypnotised by Yang or D'Onston or both of them, and that the power of the human mind to deceive was a wonder. Well, my bruises and torn suit were real enough.

"Nevertheless, you need to write your version down just as you remember it. It's for a gentleman who's very interested in this case. I'm telling you, Stubbsy, it will be to your advantage."

"Who is he? How does he know about it?"

"I can't give you a name," Arthur chided. "As to how he knows… it's ripples. Every action makes ripples on the pond, as our honourable friend from the mysterious East would say. Like in the fight game. Once a bloke wins a couple, word gets out and the fancy takes notice. Trust me, write it down."

Of course, I trust Arthur. Now, I have finished writing it all down, but the results are hardly satisfactory. I have tried to keep fact and fiction separate, though Yang might laugh at me for the attempt. I doubt how well I have succeeded; some passages leap out as dreams or hallucinations. Though perhaps hypnosis is easier to contemplate than the alternative—that such things are really possible, and the dead walk, people like D'Onston wield genuine powers, and ungodly things inhabit spaces beyond our reach.

If I knew I was going to write fiction, I could at least have written myself wiser. And wittier. I could have made myself less of a blundering oaf and more of a sharp thinker who had figured it all out from the start. I could have written myself handsome. I could have at least chopped the truth a little less close to the bone and not have my bacon being saved by a six-year-old girl who reads better than me.

I do at least understand a little more how fact and fiction work together. It's like a steak and kidney pudding: without steak, there's no substance; without kidney, there's no savour. You need the proper mixture. Pure fact is too indigestible without the imaginative part that fills in the spaces between. That's the only way to make a satisfying pudding.

But I have also begun to apprehend the dangerous power of writing. Howard died because he read Roslyn D'Onston's work and was sucked into it. Powell, too, was probably a normal enough man until he started reading detective stories and was overcome with a mania for solving the Ripper case. If Victor had taken to horticulture instead of reading Theosophy books, he would never have been harmed.

Roslyn D'Onston himself only wanted to be a magician because he read Bulwer-Lytton when he was a boy. Otherwise, maybe he'd have stuck with being a Customs officer and would never have dreamed of re-animation and human sacrifice and the rest of it.

While I am at it, maybe I should add Harry Stubbs to that list of unfortunates whose lives were derailed by reading too much of the wrong stuff. I don't see myself any closer to a decent clerical position now than I was before. Everyone knows I was in some sort of punch-up; they assume it was some business of Arthur's. It won't help my reputation.

At any rate, it's too late to change the story now. I told Arthur yesterday that it was nearly finished.

"Well done Stubbsy," he said, patting me on the shoulder. "He'll be very glad to read it."

"I still wish I knew who 'he' was and why he wants to reads it."

Arthur smiled knowingly.

"Think of it," he said, "as a job application."

Editor's Note

As usual, Harry Stubbs's account appears accurate as far as it can be checked.

Madame Helena Blavatsky, founder of modern Theosophy, lived in Maycot in Norwood while assembling her notes for *The Secret Doctrine,* "the synthesis of science, religion and philosophy," in 1887. During this time she was visited by WB Yeats. She had been accused of fakery and was widely considered to be a charlatan. During her stay her assistant, Mabel Collins, who owned the house, formed a relationship with Robert D'Onston Stephenson.

Collins came to believe that Stephenson carried out the Jack the Ripper killings in 1888, a theory supported by Aleister Crowley and explained in detail in Ivor Edwards's book *Jack the Ripper's Black Magic Rituals* (2001). The theory relies on Stephenson's own doubtful testimony.

Stephenson, who wrote under the pen name of Roslyn D'Onston, published many accounts of magic in West Africa and elsewhere. These fantastic tales appear to be fabricated for a credulous readership. His occult writings are collected in *Crowley's Ripper* (2006) at http://kobek.com/crowleyripper.pdf.

The Si Fan is a fictitious organisation, invented by Sax Rohmer for his Fu Manchu series of novels (1913-1959). The name is a typically heavy-handed joke of Stubbs's, his way of concealing the true identity of Yang's employers. Of course, no such organisation has ever existed.

Palingenesis is an alchemical process with no scientific standing and is purely pseudoscience. The only modern claim that a human can be resurrected in this way is in H. P. Lovecraft's *The Case of Charles Dexter Ward* (1927); this is now considered to be purely a work of fiction.

About the Author

David Hambling is a journalist and author who has lived in Norwood, South London since 2000. He writes about science and technology for New Scientist magazine, The Economist, WIRED, Popular Mechanics, and writes a science column for Fortean Times ("the magazine of unexplained phenomena"). In addition to non-fiction books, his "Shadows From Norwood" project seeks to bring HP Lovecraft's Cthulhu Mythos to South London, via the Harry Stubbs novels and a number of short stories.

Visit the Shadows from Norwood Facebook page :

https://www.facebook.com/ShadowsFromNorwood

...for links, photographs, interactive map and more about the Harry Stubbs Adventures series

12956605R10070

Printed in Great Britain
by Amazon